Strung Up

Also from Lorelei James

Rough Riders Series (in reading order)
LONG HARD RIDE
RODE HARD
COWGIRL UP AND RIDE
ROUGH, RAW AND READY
BRANDED AS TROUBLE
STRONG SILENT TYPE (novella)
SHOULDA BEEN A COWBOY
ALL JACKED UP
RAISING KANE
SLOW RIDE (free short story)
COWGIRLS DON'T CRY
CHASIN' EIGHT
COWBOY CASANOVA
KISSIN' TELL
GONE COUNTRY
SHORT RIDES (anthology)
REDNECK ROMEO
COWBOY TAKE ME AWAY
LONG TIME GONE (novella)

Blacktop Cowboys® Series (in reading order)
CORRALLED
SADDLED AND SPURRED
WRANGLED AND TANGLED
ONE NIGHT RODEO
TURN AND BURN
HILLBILLY ROCKSTAR
ROPED IN (novella)
STRIPPED DOWN (novella)
WRAPPED AND STRAPPED
HANG TOUGH (Nov 2016)

Mastered Series (in reading order)
BOUND
UNWOUND
SCHOOLED (digital only novella)
UNRAVELED
CAGED

Rough Riders Legacy Series
UNBREAK MY HEART

Single Title Novels
RUNNING WITH THE DEVIL
DIRTY DEEDS

Single Title Novellas
LOST IN YOU (short novella)
WICKED GARDEN
MISTRESS CHRISTMAS (Wild West Boys)
MISS FIRECRACKER (Wild West Boys)
BALLROOM BLITZ (Two To Tango anthology)

Need You Series
WHAT YOU NEED
JUST WHAT I NEEDED
ALL YOU NEED (April 2017)

Lorelei James also writes as mystery author Lori Armstrong

Strung Up

A Blacktop Cowboys® Novella

By Lorelei James

1001 Dark Nights

EVIL EYE
CONCEPTS

Strung Up
A Blacktop Cowboys® Novella
By Lorelei James

1001 Dark Nights
Copyright 2016 LJLA, LLC
ISBN: 978-1-942299-49-3

Foreword: Copyright 2014 M. J. Rose
Published by Evil Eye Concepts, Incorporated

Sign up for the 1001 Dark Nights Newsletter
and be entered to win a Tiffany Key necklace.

There's a contest every month!

Go to www.1001DarkNights.com to subscribe.

As a bonus, all subscribers will receive a free
1001 Dark Nights story
The First Night
by Lexi Blake & M.J. Rose

One Thousand and One Dark Nights

Once upon a time, in the future…

*I was a student fascinated with stories and learning.
I studied philosophy, poetry, history, the occult, and
the art and science of love and magic. I had a vast
library at my father's home and collected thousands
of volumes of fantastic tales.*

*I learned all about ancient races and bygone
times. About myths and legends and dreams of all
people through the millennium. And the more I read
the stronger my imagination grew until I discovered
that I was able to travel into the stories... to actually
become part of them.*

*I wish I could say that I listened to my teacher
and respected my gift, as I ought to have. If I had, I
would not be telling you this tale now.
But I was foolhardy and confused, showing off
with bravery.*

*One afternoon, curious about the myth of the
Arabian Nights, I traveled back to ancient Persia to
see for myself if it was true that every day Shahryar
(Persian: شهریار, "king") married a new virgin, and then
sent yesterday's wife to be beheaded. It was written
and I had read, that by the time he met Scheherazade,
the vizier's daughter, he'd killed one thousand
women.*

*Something went wrong with my efforts. I arrived
in the midst of the story and somehow exchanged
places with Scheherazade – a phenomena that had
never occurred before and that still to this day, I
cannot explain.*

*Now I am trapped in that ancient past. I have
taken on Scheherazade's life and the only way I can
protect myself and stay alive is to do what she did to
protect herself and stay alive.*

*Every night the King calls for me and listens as I spin tales.
And when the evening ends and dawn breaks, I stop at a
point that leaves him breathless and yearning for more.
And so the King spares my life for one more day, so that
he might hear the rest of my dark tale.*

*As soon as I finish a story... I begin a new
one... like the one that you, dear reader, have before
you now.*

Prologue

Cres

I believe that love is stronger than death.

That had become my mantra, my focal point in the last seven days, ten hours, and thirty-four minutes since the highway patrolman had knocked on my door.

I'm sorry to inform you that Michael Darby was involved in an accident and died at the scene. He listed you as his emergency contact.

The rest of what he'd said had been a blur.

At first I thought there'd been a mistake. Michael Darby and Mick Darby. I'd never called him Michael. He never called himself Michael. So maybe the cops had it wrong. Maybe there was another person's life they should be destroying with this bad news that their lover was dead.

So I argued.

Then the officer calmly pulled Mick's driver's license out of the leather wallet I'd given him for Christmas.

And then I knew it was true.

Mick was dead.

How could he be dead?

How was that fucking fair? He'd survived four wartime deployments overseas during his military career. Four years in hell. Only to be killed by a jack slipping and crushing him beneath the wheel of a car.

The injustice infuriated me. Mick being a good guy once again. The Samaritan who always stopped to help. Only this time his helpful nature had gotten him killed.

I wanted to yell at him for being so stupid.

But I'd never get to yell at him again. Or laugh with him. Or touch him. Or tell him I loved him.

He knew. Because you reminded him of that every day.

"Let us pray," the minister announced.

I bowed my head. But my focus wasn't on the minister's pointless platitudes. Instead I studied the shoes of the other four people in the front pew with me, all with one commonality—each pair was black. Mick's father wore polished dress cowboy boots. Mick's mother had opted for closed-toe pumps. Mick's sister Aria had chosen wedges. Mick's brother Sam had donned loafers.

I had Mick's favorite pair of boots on my feet. It'd been a joke between us that since we were the same size in clothing and footwear, we'd doubled the size of our wardrobes when he'd moved in with me.

I'd felt the need to wear him today. His boots, his socks, his belt, his T-shirt beneath his white dress shirt. The suit was mine. The tie was his.

Had been his.

Fuck. Would I ever get used to thinking of him in the past tense?

"Amen."

I raised my head.

Music played behind us. The organ made the tune nearly unrecognizable until the singer started "Let It Be" by the Beatles.

I closed my eyes. *Please be a shitty rendition that's way the fuck out of tune. Please garble the words so I can't understand them.*

But short of jamming my fingers in my ears and singing *la-la-la*...I couldn't tune it out.

It was beautifully sung. Poignant. I wouldn't cry. Not because I thought I was too tough to publicly show that I'd had my guts and my heart ripped out. But because if I started to bawl, I might not be able to stop.

Finally, the song ended.

Then the service ended.

I felt as if my world had ended.

Everyone stood as the urn was wheeled out. Now we'd make the sixty-mile drive to the veteran's cemetery in Miles City. Mick would have the military burial he deserved. Then we'd return to the Darby's house for the repast with his friends and his family that I didn't know, talking about "Michael," the man I hadn't known at all.

Outside on the sidewalk in front of the small white church, I looked up at the steeple as the bell eerily clanged a death toll. Mick's family had told me this was where Mick had been baptized and confirmed. They'd probably hoped he'd be married here. Instead he'd been eulogized.

I had a hard time wrapping my head around the fact Mick had decided on all of his funeral details prior to his first deployment. It didn't matter that ten years had passed. It didn't matter that I was his lover and partner now; I'd had no input regarding the ceremony.

What would you have done differently?

"Cres? You ready?"

I glanced at my brother Wyn. Both my brothers and their wives had driven to Montana for this, even after I'd told them they didn't have to come. But now, as I watched Mick's family climb into the limo—they claimed there was no room for me—I was glad my family was here. I wouldn't be forced to make the drive to Miles City by myself.

If you were here by yourself you wouldn't go to the cemetery. You'd jump in your truck and haul ass back to Colorado. Because Mick isn't in that urn. He won't know that you skipped out on the interment. Mick's family would rather you weren't there because then they won't have to justify why they're being handed the folded flag instead of you.

But would he have wanted me to have it? Since my presence and my role in his life had come as a shock to his family?

They believed—Mick had told them—that I was his roommate.

His fucking roommate.

The lie—his lie—had sliced a jagged cut to my soul that left a scar straight down to the bone.

I heard Mick's justification in my head as clearly as if he'd been in our bed next to me, whispering it in my ear. *What does it matter?* You *know who you are to me.* You *know what you mean to me. They are my past. You are my future.*

And so I'd forgiven him before I had a chance to be mad at him.

After today, it wouldn't matter. I'd never see Mick's family again, so I didn't give a rat's ass what they thought of me.

"Creston? Are you ready?" my mom prompted.

I shook my head. "I'm not going."

"Of course you're going, sweetheart," she said gently. "This final stage will be hard, but we're all here for you."

"Fine. You go. I'll meet you at the motel afterward. Or better yet, I'll see you at home on the ranch."

"Don't be ridiculous—"

"Sue," my father said sharply, "drop it. If he doesn't want to go, he doesn't have to go."

Having my dad's support meant everything to me. I looked at Wyn and Sutton.

They nodded in solidarity.

To keep myself from breaking down, I turned away and repeated my mantra.

I believe that love is stronger than death.

But I knew I'd never give love a chance to break me again.

Chapter One

Cres
Two years later...

"I don't see why I need to go to this thing. It has nothin' to do with me."

My brother Wyn paused long enough that I was forced to meet his gaze.

I saw a hard look in his eyes and I knew I was totally fucked.

"You *are* goin' because more than half of your family is involved in this new venture. And you will show support for it and for your brother and sisters-in-law, Cres, if I have to hogtie you, prop you up in the corner and paint a goddamned smile on your face myself."

"Fine. Whatever. I'll be there." I slapped Petey on the rump and turned him out into the pasture to graze. I hefted the saddle off the fence and hauled it inside the barn. When I returned for the saddle blanket and the rest of the tack, I saw that Wyn still rested against the corral, his arms crossed, probably waiting to rip into me some more.

I ignored him.

Wyn followed me into the tack room.

I continued to ignore him.

I took my time putting everything away in its proper place, hanging up the saddle blanket to dry before I faced him. "What? I said I'd be there."

"Good. We miss you," he said softly.

"You see me every damn day, Wyn."

He shook his head. "I work with you every day. Outside of that, we don't see you."

I turned away. "You've got your own life with Mel and your son." I didn't point out it was the same situation with our other brother Sutton, his wife London, and their little boy, Brennen. I was the odd man out—in so many ways.

"I'll pick you up at six-thirty."

"I can drive myself."

"Nope. You're goin' with me. This is not negotiable."

Anger made me snap, "I *said* I'd be there. I don't need a fucking escort."

"You brought this on yourself, Cres, since you haven't shown up for any of the other family get-togethers in the past year after you promised you would. Not takin' a chance this time. Besides, I need you to drive my truck back here. Melissa drove her car earlier today and we don't need two vehicles there since we're stayin' overnight."

"So in addition to bein' forced to attend this thing, I'll also have to stay sober?"

"Yep." Wyn moved in behind me and squeezed my shoulder. "Clean yourself up. I'll be back in an hour. Don't make me come lookin' for you."

I stayed in the barn until I heard my brother's rig drive off. Then I grabbed a beer out of the fridge and headed toward the house.

Clean yourself up. I had half a notion to stay in the same stinky-ass, manure splattered clothes I had on. Why did it matter what I wore? The shindig was being held in a barn. A three-million-dollar-barn, but a barn nonetheless.

But showing up as the dirty, bedraggled, surly brother would bring unwanted attention to me. Better to clean up, blend in, and play the part they demanded.

I stripped down as I walked through my house and was naked by the time I reached the bathroom. I stepped into the shower, letting the tepid water run over me for a long time. It'd been a hot and dusty day moving cattle and the cool water felt good. Keeping my eyes closed, I remained under the spray as I finished my beer. Then I grabbed the soap and lathered up. Rinsed off. Dried off. As I shaved, I figured any day now my mom would say I needed a haircut. Maybe I oughta just grow a beard and go with the whole mountain-man look.

Don't you mean hermit?

Standing in front of my closet as I towel dried my hair, I scowled at my clothing selection. They'd better not expect me to wear a damn suit.

My stomach bottomed out when I remembered the last time I'd worn one.

Mick's funeral.

Blindly, I thrust my hand into the closet and grabbed a long-sleeved shirt. I slipped it on over my T-shirt and tucked it into my jeans. Belt on, boots on, dress hat by the door, I snagged another beer and parked myself on the couch to wait for my babysitter to arrive.

* * * *

Wyn arrived on time.

After I hopped into the passenger side, I turned around to look in the back of the double cab, expecting to see my nephew Evan happily kicking his chubby legs in his car seat. But the car seat was empty. "Where's the rug rat?" I asked my brother.

"Mom and Dad are watching him and Brennen."

Brennen, Sutton and London's son, was only two months younger than Evan. Our folks were in heaven with their two adorable grandsons. "So they get to skip this event? Shoot, if I'da known that was an option, I would've volunteered to babysit."

He snorted. "Standin' around sipping beer and listening to speeches is a cakewalk compared to chasin' after a couple of two-year-olds. Consider yourself lucky."

"How long is this thing supposed to last?"

"No idea. They invited like a thousand people."

That shocked me. "A thousand people? Jesus. Why so many?"

"Grade A Farms jumping into the rodeo school arena is a big damn deal. You oughta know by now that the Gradskys don't do anything half-assed."

"When does the rodeo school open officially?"

"Next month, I guess. They're workin' out the scheduling since they'll have to utilize all three arenas on the property. They're already near full capacity for enrollment. I'm betting that after tonight they'll have a waiting list. They keep expanding operations and they'll own the entire southeastern corner of Colorado."

The Gradskys' main chunk of land, Grade A Farms, devoted to

raising rodeo stock—both rodeo rough stock and horse breeding—was a hundred miles south of the Grant Ranch. "Why'd they build the school this far north? Wouldn't it be easier to have the breeding stock in the same place as they were teaching students?"

Wyn shot me an odd look. "Have you been payin' attention at all the past year and a half?"

I bristled. "What do you mean?"

"Gradskys relocated all their operations to this location."

"Everything?"

"Everything."

Shit. I hadn't been paying attention. "Why?"

"They outgrew the land faster than they'd planned. Plus, after London and Sutton gave Chuck and Berlin their first grandchild, they wanted to live closer. Their son Macon practices law in Denver anyway. And Stirling..."

"What's goin' on with Stirling?"

"She quit her fancy job and bought two hundred acres adjacent to her folks' place. Crazy girl has started an organic farm."

I frowned. "We're talkin' about Stirling Gradsky, right? The corporate executive is giving up power lunches in Lear jets to dig in the dirt like a common farmer?"

Wyn grinned at me. "Oh, don't kid yourself that it'll bother her to ruin her manicure. She's savvy enough to hire all the right people. But she's a control freak and has no problem doin' the dirty work so she keeps more of the profits."

"What's she growing?"

"Pot. Wish I'd thought of that," Wyn groused. "Now those commercial Ag permits are hard to come by. She skated in with all the applications the week that pot became legal in Colorado. She's gonna make a fuck-ton of money."

"Rather see her successful at it than these out-of-state fuckers."

"Amen."

"What did the Gradskys do with their other place? Sell it?"

Wyn shook his head. "Kept it. Turned it into a full-time cattle operation and a dude ranch. The Gradskys' nephews Lewis and Clark are running it. They're good guys. I feel bad their folks saddled them with those names. You met them at Sutton and London's wedding. But maybe you don't remember."

I didn't. Because I met someone far more important than them: Mick.

I got really quiet.

"What?"

"You're right. I haven't been paying attention to anything. It's just…" How did I say this? "Why haven't you all given up on me?"

"Because you're family, bro. All we can do is be here for you when you're ready to pay attention again."

I scrubbed my hands over my face. "If I haven't said so, I appreciate that none of you have nagged and told me I've been grieving long enough and it's time to move on."

Wyn actually looked horrified. "Cres, that ain't for anybody but you to decide. I wasn't bullshitting you earlier. We miss you. All of us do. We thought it'd do us all good to be together tonight, no kids, no talkin' about the ranch. Just the five of us hanging out."

I tried not to think back when it was the six of us hanging out. My brothers and their wives had accepted Mick and me as a couple and him as part of the family. "It still feels wrong that he's not here," I admitted.

My brother reached over and patted my leg.

The drive had taken a little more than half an hour. We turned down a dirt road and I saw hundreds of cars parked in a field off to the left side.

"Holy shit."

"I had that same reaction the first time I saw it too. Like I said, the Gradskys don't do anything half-assed. They arranged for buses to take guests up to the compound."

Berlin and Chuck Gradsky were my sister-in-law London's parents. Their business interests ran the gamut from horse breeding, to horse training, to cattle ranching, and they invested their all financially and personally in every venture they attempted, which was why it seemed everything they touched turned to gold. After Sutton became their son-in-law, Wyn and I became part of their family too. I'd understood why Wyn was in the inner Gradsky loop, since his wife Melissa worked as a teacher and a trainer for Grade A. But they'd accepted me too—welcomed me even—and that meant more than I could express.

Wyn bypassed the parking lot. He handed me a heavy piece of paper he'd pulled down from his sun visor. "VIP parking pass. Put that on the dash."

It was hard not to gawk at the structures as we tooled up the blacktop. We passed three indoor arenas, each with its own corral. The road forked and a sign marked "dormitories" pointed to the right. Behind the trees I could make out two buildings with a courtyard between them. The road split again and an arrow pointed to the left with a sign that read "classrooms and dining hall." Then we crested a rise. I blinked at what appeared to be a small town spread out at the base of the hill.

"They did all of this in a year and a half?"

"Actually, it's been less than a year."

"Did you know the Gradskys had this kind of money?"

He shook his head. "I don't think anyone knew, including their kids."

"Well, everyone will know after tonight, won't they?"

"Yep." Wyn parked in the VIP lot.

We hoofed it through the tall grass toward the biggest tent I'd ever seen—guess a three-million-dollar barn wasn't big enough to hold everyone. Beneath the big top were bleachers. I half-expected to see clowns making balloon animals, jugglers throwing flaming batons into the air, scantily clad women twirling on trapezes, and the trumpeting of elephants.

I muttered, "I need a damn drink."

"Staff and family have their own section with an open bar. We're almost there."

The moment we stepped through the curtained-off area, my sister-in-law Melissa threw herself at my brother, greeting him with a steamy kiss. Then she whapped him on the chest. "What took you so long?"

"I checked on Evan before I picked Cres up."

Melissa whirled around, noticing me for the first time.

I managed a smile at her look of shock that I'd actually shown up. "Hey, Mel. You're lookin'—"

"Round. I wasn't this big at the end of my last pregnancy." Then she wrapped herself around me as best as she could with the basketball baby between us. "I'm so glad you're here, Cres."

"I appreciate the invite. How are you really feelin', little mama?"

"I'm excited for everyone to see the facility. It's been crazy today, running all over the place, getting everything ready."

Wyn loomed over her as soon as she stepped away from me. "When was the last time you sat down?"

"I don't know. I'm fine. Stop fussing."

"Like that's gonna happen. Your ankles are swollen. You need to be off your feet until this shindig is underway."

His tone meant business. Mel's diabetes added to my brother's worries and she knew better than to argue.

"We're sitting at the far back table since it's closest to the bathroom."

"Let's go."

I trudged behind them. As soon as Wyn reached the table, he plopped down and scooped Mel onto his lap, kicking out a chair for her to put her feet up on. I made a beeline for the bar. I ordered two Fat Tires and brought one back to him.

"Thanks."

Mel toasted with her bottle of water. "London and Sutton will be along any minute."

"What time does this start?"

"The official program and introduction of the instructors begins at eight. Tours have been underway since about four."

"Now I wish we would've gotten here earlier," I said, surprising myself and them. "I'd like to check it all out."

"I'll give you a personal tour any time you want," London said behind me. Then she wrapped her arms around my shoulders and squeezed me tight. "So, so, so glad you came, Cres."

"Me, too."

My brother Sutton dropped into the chair next to mine. Not only was I the youngest of the Grant boys, at six feet two and one hundred eighty pounds, I was also the runt of the litter. Both Sutton and Wyn topped me by two inches.

Sutton's way of saying hello was to grin at me before he swiped my beer. "Thanks."

Some things never changed.

I got up to get another beer and just to be ornery, brought London back a double shot of tequila. London tended to get out of hand once the tequila started flowing and it was my right to encourage it on a night of celebration.

"Ooh, you read my mind, Cres. Thanks," London said and touched the plastic glass to my beer bottle before she downed the shot.

I said, "You're welcome."

"Really, Cres?" Sutton complained.

Wyn laughed. "You brought that one on yourself."

"Yeah," I retorted. "Next time, get your own damn beer."

And then it really did seem like old times. As if it'd just been last week that we'd all hung out, shooting the breeze and drinking beer. I even managed to laugh when London launched into a story about horse training that somehow shifted to potty training Brennen.

But our family time ended all too soon. Before I had time to ready myself for being in a crowd, we were surrounded by one. The Gradskys descended. Berlin hugged me, Chuck and Macon shook my hand, followed by a reintroduction to London's cousins who were running the dude ranch. That group expanded to include all the employees and their spouses until it seemed a hundred people were crammed into the space, all talking at once.

Would anyone notice if I snuck out?

Doubtful.

I sucked it up and stayed until Berlin and Chuck took center stage.

The crowd beneath the big top quieted as the introductions of the instructors began. I half-listened because I recognized knew a few names from the world of rodeo anyway.

When the lines opened to the buffet, the crush of people made it hard to breathe. I slipped out the back, the opposite direction of the food line. I'd never been one for crowds and after spending the last two years in isolation, this scene sent me searching for solitude.

A white catering van had been parked near the rear exit. It appeared I wasn't the only one seeking an escape. A big guy, roughly the same size as Sutton, rested against the side of the van, one boot heel hooked to the running board. He wore dark jeans and a plain white button down shirt with a logo on the left pocket. He'd angled his head down, obscuring his face. But with that build and that posture, I knew I was looking at a rodeo cowboy.

Something seemed familiar about him.

That's when I noticed the poker chip in his left hand. He passed it through his fingers over and over again. I recognized that nervous tic.

My gut tightened. I took a few more steps forward, alerting him to my presence.

He palmed the poker chip before he slowly raised his head and looked at me.

Then I was staring into that face. That handsome fucking smug face.

A face I used to dream of.

A face I hadn't seen in four years, since Sutton and London's wedding.

I waited for the dismissive sneer to distort that perfect mouth.

A mouth I'd dreamed of nearly as often as his perfect face.

But no sneer formed.

His compelling eyes met mine.

I saw his recognition in those arctic blue depths. Followed by wariness. But no hardness. Or the mean glint I'd unconsciously steeled myself against.

He didn't move.

Neither did I.

I found my voice. "Breck?"

"Hey, Cres."

"What are you doin' out here?"

"Same thing you're doin', I reckon. Avoiding the crowd." He paused and dipped his chin to the empty space beside him. "There's room if you wanna take a load off."

I waited for the innuendo.

None came.

Everything inside me cautioned me to beat a fast retreat.

Not everything. My long-dormant libido urged me to stay.

Chapter Two

Breck

I watched Creston Grant trying to decide whether to stay or go.

I didn't blame him for his indecision.

The Breck he remembered? Total fucking tool. As well as being a world-class asshole, a condescending prick, a sharp-tongued dickhead, and a douchebag.

Yeah, I'd been the posterchild for how *not* to win friends and influence people.

Little wonder I was back here hiding, wondering what the hell I'd gotten myself into again.

Cres heaved a sigh and shuffled forward. Then he turned and planted his backside next to mine—but not too close to mine.

I quietly exhaled.

He didn't speak right away. I remembered that about him—he weighed his words carefully before he spoke. At first I'd believed it was a family trait he shared with his brother Sutton, the stereotypical quiet gruff cowboy. But then I discovered the reason for his caution—his sexual orientation. I might be in a different situation if I'd acted more circumspect.

But I also remembered finding a fissure in that tough outer shell of his. And how easy it was to apply the perfect amount of pressure until that fissure widened into a crack—a crack I used to open him up fully to all the naked possibilities between us. I should've felt guilty; Cres was a decade younger and hadn't built up defenses against a guy like me. Yet, of all my conquests, Cres Grant had been the one I'd regretted letting go.

"I'm surprised to see you back here alone," he said, interrupting my silent contemplation. "I thought you preferred to be in the thick of things."

"I used to."

"What changed?"

"Everything."

"That's cryptic."

"It is what it is."

From the corner of my eye I saw Cres turn his head and squint at me. "So why are you here, Breck?"

"Here in Colorado at the grand opening of Grade A Rodeo Academy?"

He nodded.

"Sutton, London, or Mel didn't fill you in?" I asked.

"Nope. I've been out of the loop since…" He paused. "For a while."

I shoved the poker chip in my front jeans pocket. "I remember you tellin' me you didn't follow rodeo even when your brother dominated the leaderboard."

Cres shrugged. "Not my thing. So you're here as a guest?"

"Nah. I'm a staff member."

He frowned. "I didn't hear your name called or see you go up to the podium when Chuck and Berlin introduced the staff."

"That's because I asked to remain anonymous."

"Right. Because you're still way too fucking cool for all this bullshit."

His response wasn't unexpected but it still stung. The old me would've gone off on him, belittling him, berating him until he slunk away with his tail between his legs, allowing me to feel superior. I didn't have it in me to be that guy anymore.

"Yeah. That's it. You've got me pegged." I pushed away from the van. "Nice seein' you, Cres. Take care." I skirted the front end of the van and kept walking along the raised ledge of the small ravine until the noise faded and I could breathe.

Heedless of the dusty surface, I found a flat spot and let my feet dangle over the edge. Wasn't a huge drop, but it'd be a bitch to climb out of if I slipped. Good thing I hadn't been drinking. Scooping up a handful of rocks, I thought about the last time I'd seen Cres—at Sutton and London's wedding. So much of that time was a blur of booze. I'd managed to scrounge up a date because back then it'd been paramount to keep up appearances.

Nothing to see over here, folks. Just a horny single cowboy adding a new notch on his championship belt by bedding yet another hot woman.

I'd had a huge ego back then too. It'd been heady stuff, knowing guys wanted to be me; on fire in the arena and burning up the sheets with a different buckle bunny every night.

But it'd all been a lie. A house of cards about to tumble and crush me like a bug.

I might've been able to survive rumors of fucking anything with a pulse if I'd had a winning season. In previous years, officials, sponsors, and even rodeo fans chalked up the rumors of my insatiable sexual appetite as blowing off steam after my many wins. The whispers of my sexcapades with same-sex partners were written off as drunken experimentation after too many Jäger shots. Even the wildest rumors worked to my advantage and added to my status that I could have any woman I wanted on her knees with just a look.

Problem was it wasn't a woman I wanted on her knees.

When I began to lose on the circuit, the females I'd counted on to flock around me as camouflage began to flit away. I should've become more cautious at that point, not more reckless. Somehow I believed my oversized championship belt buckle had become a shield. That I was invincible. Impervious. That with three All-Around world titles I could be forgiven anything.

Wrong.

When you're on the highest rung of the ladder, hitting the bottom leaves you far more broken than you ever imagined.

It'd been a long, slow recovery and no climb back to the top. And for me, there'd been no privacy while I dealt with the various traumas—physical and mental. There'd been no one to lean on, no one to talk to.

That had been the reality of my life the past three years. Humbled and lonely.

I tossed a pebble at a flat rock and watched it bounce down into the ravine.

Boot steps shuffled behind me.

Had I really thought he'd let me go without poking his nose into my business?

You were hoping he wouldn't.

Cres crouched next to me. "What happened to you?"

"Depends on who you ask," I said.

"I'm askin' you, Breck."

I turned my head and met his gaze. Brown eyes the color of cinnamon stared back at me. I let my focus drift over Cres's face. Damn man still had the power to render me incoherent. All those rugged angles that made up his face epitomized magnificent. Seeing his curiosity and not pity allowed me to say, "Pull up a rock."

He shifted from a crouch into a sitting position. "You couldn't have stormed off to a table by the bar instead of the edge of a cliff?"

"I didn't storm off," I retorted. "And it's hardly a cliff."

"I remember you always had a flair for drama."

"I've had enough drama to last a lifetime." I shot him a sideways glance. "And if you use the word *queen*, I'm pushing you over the edge."

"Whoa." Cres put up his hands in mock surrender. "Never crossed my mind. So am I the only person at the open house that doesn't have a freakin' clue as to what's goin' on with you?"

"Probably. In the words of the reporter who wrote the article, 'this story rocked the very foundation of the rodeo community.'"

"That bad, huh? What'd you do? Shoot a jealous lover in self-defense or something?"

I snorted. "Sad to say I'd be forgiven for that. Really sad to think that homicide is preferable to bein' a homosexual in the pro rodeo world."

That admission startled him. "That's what's goin' on with you? Jesus. I had no idea." He paused and studied me.

"No one did."

Cres reached for a small rock and chucked it at the other side, sending up a puff of dirt. "What made you decide to come out?"

"I didn't. The decision was taken out of my hands."

"Really? How?"

"Cockiness on my part. I'd been seeing this guy Carlyle off and on. He wasn't part of the rodeo scene so I thought I was safe. He knew I was in the closet and he seemed fine with it…until he wasn't. He hated the bunnies, even when nothin' was happening between them and me. He went from waitin' for me in the motel room to waitin' for me outside the stock pens. And if I tried to dodge him, well, he cranked the gay on high and threw a major sissy-hissy fit. To make matters worse, I had the shittiest run of my career. I wasn't even in the top twenty in my circuit. So

I broke it off with him, telling him I needed to concentrate on getting back on top—which wasn't exactly a lie. I thought he understood what was at stake for me. I thought he'd keep his mouth shut and move on."

"What'd he do?"

"Called *Country Times Today* magazine, that piece of crap rag devoted to gossip in the country music scene that also regularly reports on CRA and EBS standings. Carlyle spilled his guts and my secrets, all in the guise of helping us find our way back to each other because he believed 'our love shouldn't have to be hidden away.'" Yeah. No sarcasm there.

"Lemme guess. This guy was a pretty-boy model type? From one of the coasts?" Cres said with a sneer in his tone.

I couldn't even bristle at that presumption because he'd hit it right on. "Everyone has a type. A pretty boy happens to be mine." I started to remind Cres that's why he and I had hooked up—his pretty face with those high cheekbones, chiseled jawline, aristocratic nose, and full lips did it for me in a bad way. The passing years had just fine-tuned his features and he'd grown from a pretty boy into a beautiful man.

"So the country tattler printed the story and then...?"

My neck and face burned hot, as it always did whenever I thought about the day my life as I'd known it had ended. "It wasn't just a small paragraph buried in the back of the rodeo stats page. I'd scored the front cover and an eight-page spread with other 'secret male lovers' coming forward. Christ. They even had pictures. One picture in particular of me and Carlyle in bed. I was asleep with my head on his chest, so I had no fucking idea he'd even taken it.

"I'd finally started winning again and that's why I thought there were a bunch of reporters waitin' for me after I'd won the tie-down and bulldoggin' events in Prescott. The appearance of the article completely blindsided me. As did all the questions about my perversions as a liar and a sodomite who'd hopped on the express train to hell."

He whistled.

"Yeah. And it gets better. Although I never figured out which one of my competitors had a hand in getting the article published, all the rest of them took advantage of running me down when the AP got ahold of the story. The national news services interviewed anyone who would talk smack about me—which was everyone. Guys I'd never met claimed they'd always known something was 'off' with me. Each quote was another blow, knocking me so deep into the dirt..." *I feared I'd never dig myself out*. I paused and swallowed hard. "Not a single person on the circuit stood up for me, Cres. Not one. I'd been friends with some of them for a decade. I'd helped them out professionally. Several of the guys…I'd been at their ranches workin' as a hand during calving and branding. I knew their wives and their kids and they all turned their backs on me."

"Man. That is harsh. I'm sorry. I don't know what else to say."

"Most people thought I got what I had coming to me. There was talk for a few months of the CRA stripping me of my world titles. It never happened, but my name was tarnished beyond repair at that point anyway. My sponsors dropped me. The rodeo organizations, even at the county level, banned me from competing. People laugh about bein' blackballed, but it is a very real and a very ugly thing." I couldn't admit to him that even the "rainbow" circuit for gay cowboys wouldn't have me because I refused to publicly state my sexual orientation.

"What'd you do?"

"Went home to South Dakota. Or I tried to go home. My brother was waitin' for me at the end of the road, blocking me from stepping foot on the family farm. He didn't say a word to me when he handed me the paper that cut all ties and connections to the Christianson family."

"You're fucking kiddin' me."

I shook my head. "Mom and Dad, my brothers and my sister—they disowned me. They wrote letters denouncing me and had them notarized and everything. The last bit of paperwork denied me any future claim whatsoever on any part of the Christianson farm or the land despite the fact I'd sunk three quarters of a million dollars into keeping it afloat over the years. Since they were family, I never asked for a legal contract, so I was fucked."

"Didn't the magazine at least give you a chance to tell your side of the story? Or interview you?"

"Nope. They told the story as they saw fit. The following month they'd moved on to something else. By then, I had no choice but to move on because the article had destroyed my life as I knew it. I lost everything."

"What happened to the Carlyle guy who sold the story to the magazine?" he demanded.

"He left me a voice mail full of self-righteousness, pointing out I'd brought everything on myself by denying my true nature."

"That wasn't for him to decide."

"True. But he wasn't wrong. Maybe everything would've blown up in my face eventually. It just happened sooner rather than later." I knocked my shoulder into his. "Enough about me. What's goin' on with you?"

Cres stiffened up. "Not much. Ranching with Wyn."

"That's it?"

"Yep." His face fell into shadow when he lowered his head and focused on brushing the dust off his jeans.

"I pour my guts out about the shitshow that my life has become and 'not much, ranching with Wyn' is all I get from you? Fuck that, Cres. Do they know—?"

"That I'm gay? Yeah. I came out after Sutton and London got together."

Something about that timeframe sparked a memory. "A few months after we hooked up in Denver?"

"Yep." Cres fastened his gaze to mine. "It's because of you that I had the balls to start that 'I'm gay' conversation with them."

"Why?" Hopefully I hadn't given him some stupid drunken speech about honesty when I hadn't been honest with myself about who I was until I'd been forced into it.

"Because I didn't want to live my life like you."

My jaw tightened.

"Don't get me wrong," he said apologetically. "I know why you chose that. In a sport like rodeo where the motto is 'God and country first,' bein' openly gay just ain't done. Not surprised you didn't have any support when you were outed; more than a few guys on the circuit were probably sweating bullets that they'd be found out too."

"I was so goddamned angry about the breach of privacy that I'm ashamed to admit I considered takin' some of them that I'd been with over the years down with me."

"But you didn't, did you?" he asked alarmingly.

I shook my head. "How would takin' their choice away make me any different than what Carlyle did to me?"

Cres seemed relieved. And surprised.

Because I acted like a decent person? At one time I'd been proud of my asshole reputation. No wonder I'd isolated myself.

"Anyway, back to you. Did anything else besides seein' me livin' a lie prompt you to come out?"

"I'd gotten tired of the fix ups. Tired of women coming onto me and creating excuses about why I wasn't interested. Tired of the questions about when I planned to settle down. I wanted to be done pretending."

"You showed more maturity than I did. At an earlier age than I did."

"Yeah. Well, we're all different." He readjusted his hat.

Even a basic compliment still made him squirm and that just got to me. And charmed the hell out of me.

"Was there any fallout from the women you'd been linked to?"

"I'd only had two girlfriends during my years on the circuit who could be considered long term. They both knew I preferred dick and had their own agenda as to why they let me use them as cover. Celia Lawson—Celia Gilchrist now—wanted to build a reputation for bein' wild. And Lally Bunker…" I smirked. "She happily joined in threesomes—as long as it involved girl-on-girl time for her. So I got the rep for demanding girl-on-girl action from the bunnies chasin' after me, which worked as cover for both of us."

Cres studied me. "That week we spent together, you told me you were bisexual."

I rubbed the back of my neck and gave a sheepish chuckle. "I was an idiot, okay? I thought if I said it enough times then maybe I'd start to believe it. It would've been an easier road, refuting the 'you're gay' accusations by telling people I liked sexual variety and hated sexual labels."

"You still could've taken that tack after the article released," he pointed out.

"But like *you* said, I wanted to be done pretending. So your family was okay with you when you told them about batting for the other team?"

"They were surprised, but it didn't change anything. I still had a job on the ranch. A home near them. And yeah, I do know how lucky I am to have that family support when I hear that others don't. So speaking of family…" Cres stood. "I'd probably better get back to the party. My brothers will wonder why I disappeared again." He offered his hand to help me up.

"Thanks."

Cres pulled a little too hard and I nearly knocked him over when I popped to my feet. I kept ahold of his hand and circled my arm around his lower back to steady him.

At that moment a breeze from the ravine eddied around us, gifting me with a whiff of his skin and the lime scent of his shaving cream. During our time together in Denver, I spent hours kissing and nuzzling that strong jawline and the smooth contour of his throat. Now, with my hand on his strong back and his scent beckoning me, I wanted to haul that hard body against mine and surround myself with him.

Maybe only your dick is hard right now. Maybe this lust is one-sided.

But Cres tilted his head back, almost as if he was offering me a taste of his mouth or his throat and murmured, "You're not as heavy as I remember."

The heat in his eyes when straight to my balls. "No need to maintain all that bulk if I'm not usin' it to take down a steer."

"How is it that less looks good on you?" he said huskily.

My eyes searched his. I liked what I saw when I looked at him— eagerness, which hit the perfect mark between shy and sexy. "You flirting with me, Cres?"

He blushed and tried to retreat. "That isn't why I followed you."

I softened my stance and my tone. I didn't want to scare him away. "Why did you follow me?"

"To apologize for making assumptions about you. I understand probably more than anyone that people do change."

There was another thing I remembered about him that I'd found so damn appealing besides that muscular body honed by honest labor—a genuine sweetness. "I appreciate you sayin' that."

"Besides, it's been so long for me, I'm pretty sure I've forgotten how to flirt."

"Trust me, you're doin' fine." I cocked my head. "But you have changed."

"I ditched the passive persona."

Cres was so freaking intense with the way he studied me and my reaction to his declaration. "You weren't passive with me."

"But I wasn't assertive either."

"Is that how you are now? Assertive?"

He waited a beat to make sure he had my full attention when he said, "Very."

Fuck. Me. That one word. That determined look proved time hadn't cooled the red-hot attraction between us.

The head in my pants urged me to step forward, but the head on my shoulders resisted, reminding me that I'd learned the hard way not to make the first move.

"You couldn't have gotten ugly and bitter after your forced coming out? Let yourself go to hell?" he said lightly.

I laughed. "I'm sorry you're disappointed."

"I'm not." Cres gave me a very thorough once-over. "So not. You still pack one helluva sexual punch, Breck."

When our gazes clashed again, I said "fuck it" to myself about not making the first move. I inched closer. "Did you come to this open house alone?"

"I rode with Wyn."

"That's not what I meant."

He jammed his hands in the back pockets of his jeans and admitted, "I'm here solo."

"You're not involved with anyone?"

"Nope."

The relief I felt must've shown because Cres smirked. "Are you?"

"As you can imagine I've developed some serious trust issues, so no."

"Then I'm glad I came," he said huskily. "Even if it was too late to take any of the tours."

I tipped my head toward the arena. "I could show you around the complex if you want."

"Sure. If you don't mind stopping at the food tent first. I skipped out on supper."

"I oughta check in anyway and see if there's anything I'm supposed to be doin'."

We started walking, close enough that our shoulders nearly brushed. I'd missed this zing of sexual tension. The spark of attraction that crackled below the surface, ready to ignite at any moment. The silence between us allowed me to hear his rapid breathing and for him to hear mine. I couldn't help but sneak looks at him. That long, lean body. That strong profile nearly hidden beneath the shadow of his hat. I wanted to reacquaint myself with every hard muscle, tease every soft spot that made him growl and groan, beg and buck.

Cres stopped. His head slowly came up and our eyes connected.

"Wait here for me?" I asked.

For a moment when he hesitated, I thought he'd changed his mind.

"I'll grab some food. Come find me when you're done."

Chapter Three

Cres

I kept my head down, my focus firmly on my boots eating up the dusty ground as I headed toward the smaller tent.

What are you doing, Cres? This isn't smart.

Maybe it wasn't, but making plans with Breck didn't feel wrong.

Probably nothing would happen anyway.

Whatever you want to happen, can happen. Especially with him.

That wasn't an arguable point, so even my brain didn't bother to try and counter it.

One thing about Breck Christianson hadn't changed; the man was hot as hell. That coal black hair. Those piercing blue eyes. That mouth.

Christ that mouth could do me in. Seemed I couldn't look away from it regardless if Breck was sporting a smile or a sneer. Lust hit me with another one-two punch when I recalled how those full lips alternated between being cushiony soft, skating down my torso, or hard and firm during a breath-stealing kiss. Or a combination of both when he worked my cock over.

It'd been ages since I'd thought about that week I'd spent with him in Denver. After Sutton's career-ending rodeo injury, he'd been searching for a buyer for his temperamental—but highly prized—horse, Dial. As my brother's rodeo buddy, Breck had offered to give Dial a trial run and I'd volunteered to take the horse to the stock show.

I hadn't expected my brother's big-time rodeo buddy to be into guys.

I really hadn't expected a charismatic guy who looked like Breck to be into *me*.

Around my twenty-first birthday, I'd accepted my attraction to men wasn't a phase and that actually made me…gay. By age twenty-four I hadn't come out of the closet. I'd been cautious with hookups, sticking with blowjobs and hand jobs. I'd fucked a couple of guys and had let a couple fuck me. Pretty straightforward stuff.

Then I'd met Breck.

He'd taken my carnal education to a whole other level. It'd been an eye opener for me, experiencing that kind of deep passion and intimacy with another man. It'd given me hope that someday I'd find that same connection again, but something permanent I could be open about.

The last time I'd seen Breck had been at my brother Sutton's wedding. He'd shown up with a date—she was trashy and he was testy and surly with everyone. Even my sister-in-law mentioned Breck was quickly running out of friends on the circuit due to his recent attitude and actions.

At the time I'd wondered how much longer he could continue to live the lie. I'd intended to take him aside and try and get him to open up to me, but that night my father had suffered a near-fatal heart attack. And much later that night, I'd ended up with Mick.

My body flushed hot with guilt. I'd never told Mick about Breck. It hadn't seemed relevant. Breck had been a sexual mentor. That was it. And after Mick and I were a couple, I hadn't thought about Breck at all.

Maybe that's why you haven't told Breck about Mick either.

More guilt kicked in. Telling Breck about the death of my lover and that I'd spent the last two years in a fog would definitely put a damper on tonight's possibilities. I still wasn't sure if I could be with another man.

But wouldn't Breck be the perfect guy to test out that theory on?

"Cres?"

I glanced up and realized London's sister, Stirling, was standing in front of me. "Hey. Sorry. My mind was elsewhere." I smiled at her. "I hoped I'd get to see you since I heard you were living in the area and had become a farmer—which I see is a lie because you are not rockin' the overalls."

Standoffish Stirling actually hugged me and laughed. "It's true. I feel like a different person after I tossed off the shackles of corporate America. I've gone completely country, back to my roots."

I gave her bohemian outfit—jeans covered in rhinestones and a sheer, floral top—a quick once-over and whistled. "Overalls or not, farmer looks good on you." Stirling was one of those tall, willowy Nordic blondes with an icy outer demeanor that scared off most men. She and I had always gotten along great because I wanted nothing from her except friendship.

She kept a hold of my arm and squeezed my biceps. "Ranching has always looked good on you, Creston Grant. Are you sure you're gay? Because a dude with your looks and physique should definitely reproduce."

Just then Breck sauntered in on the other side of the tent.

Our eyes met.

Heat from his hungry look rolled through me in a wave of want so strong I had to lock my knees.

Yeah, sweetheart. I am one hundred percent about the dick.

"Have you eaten?" Stirling said. "I got stuck waiting for Liam the Lab Loser to show up and missed the chow line."

"Actually, I was headed that direction."

"Let's dine together." She looped her arm though mine.

I felt Breck's eyes on us. I could almost feel his impatience pulsing through the air.

It won't hurt him to wait a little longer. And it'll make you seem less desperate.

So I remained fully aware of Breck pacing on the other side of the tent as I loaded up a plate.

However, Stirling was blissfully unaware of the way my pulse jumped every time my gaze connected with Breck's. Or the coiled tension in every inch of my body as I imagined his rough-skinned hands gripping my ass as I thrust my cock into that Hoover of a mouth of his.

"You are starving," Stirling said as we sat at an empty picnic table. "You just made a growling noise."

I forced my gaze away from Breck and concentrated on chatting with London's little sister. "So who is this Liam guy? And why did you call him a lab loser?"

Stirling sighed and signaled to the bartender closest to us. Immediately a server dropped off two Fat Tire beers.

Handy to be dining with one of the Gradsky princesses.

"I've spent the last seven years literally working in the corporate meat market, using my animal science degree to breed better beef cattle on a large-scale commercial level without growth hormones."

A concept I was familiar with since we didn't use growth hormones.

"Now I've partnered with my brother Macon and we've jumped into the organic farming market."

I said, "What organics are you growing?" even when I already knew.

"Marijuana, man. It's what all the cool farmers are doing."

I snorted.

"But seriously, only three quarters of our total acreage will be devoted to pot. The rest is slated for organic vegetable production, concentrating on 'heritage varieties' that haven't been crossbred."

"I knew that cold, corporate hard-ass persona of yours was totally fake." I pointed at her with my beer bottle. "I always suspected you secretly wanted to be a professional pothead."

"Busted." Stirling smirked at me. "What kind of farmer doesn't regularly perform quality control tests on their crops?"

"So this Liam dude is in charge of quality control in the lab and he's blocking your access to product testing?"

"Not hardly. Dr. Liam is my brother's former client, supposedly a brilliant Ag bio-engineer and our secret weapon in advanced splicing technology. But he lives in his own little bubble. He doesn't write anything down. He doesn't follow instructions. He's conceited. And he's utterly lacking in any social graces. Lucky me has been tasked with teaching him to be a team player."

"I take it he's resistant?"

She rolled her eyes. "He's a know-it-all jackass with an IQ of like a billion but he is incapable of learning basic clerical duties. He refuses to even try."

"Did you try getting high with him and see if that mellows him out?"

"Twice. When that didn't work I even tried to bribe him with a five-hundred-dollar bottle of scotch." She shook her head. "No go there either."

"I'm guessing money isn't a factor since you probably pay him plenty."

"We pay him a fuck-ton. So that left me with sex as an incentive. I hired this super-sweet, super-smart, super-hot college student with a porn-star mouth and a pair of DD's."

For the first time ever, stick-in-the-mud Stirling reminded me of her wilder older sister London. "How'd that go?"

"The woman might as well have been wearing a sackcloth and ashes or a nun's habit for all the attention he paid to her," she complained.

I laughed.

"Cres. This is not funny. This is part of what's holding up production. Neither his formulas nor his gene splicing technique can be a secret from *us*. We need the ability to recreate in case something happened to him."

Keeping my attention on Breck, I pressed my lips to my bottle of beer and took a big swig, swallowing thickly and making a show of licking my lips when I finished.

His wicked smile promised retribution.

Bring it.

"Cres. Are you even listening to me?" Stirling demanded. "I need your help."

I refocused after discreetly readjusting the crotch of my jeans. "What can I do? High-grade pot didn't work, booze didn't work, dangling a juicy, young coed didn't work—"

"Maybe because I dangled the wrong *flavor* of juicy coed," she said. "Maybe he prefers beefcake."

Now she had my full attention. "Are you suggesting that I—"

"Show up in the lab wearing a pair of running shorts with your bare chest and abs glistening with sweat? Absolutely."

I choked on my drink of beer.

"I just need you to recheck my gaydar."

Before I could answer, a tray slammed down on the table.

Stirling's eyes widened.

A tall, lanky man stood next to me, his posture regal. If he hadn't worn a lab coat and glasses, I never would've guessed him to be an academic. He hit the mark between a hipster and an indie rocker, seriously freakin' hot in that nerdy way with his dark brown hair secured in a ponytail at the base of his neck.

"I assure you, Miss Gradsky, there is nothing wrong with your gaydar. I am entirely heterosexual." He turned and pinned me with eyes that reminded me of quicksilver. Then he offered me his hand and tight smile. "Dr. Liam Argent."

His heavily tattooed hand was smooth and his grip strong. "Cres Grant."

"Pleased to make your acquaintance, Mr. Grant. And if I had any inclination toward a dalliance on the other side of the fence, so to speak,

I'd be more than happy to see you in my lab, half-naked and glistening with sweat."

"Uh. Thanks?"

Dr. Liam angled forward so he had Stirling's full attention. "You know my conditions for taking clerical instructions, Miss Gradsky. *You* are the one who has refused to comply with the terms."

"Because I am not taking dictation as your personal secretary, dickhead," she retorted.

Yep. That response totally reminded me of London.

"It's not as if I demanded you wear thigh highs and stilettos with a Catholic schoolgirl outfit as you're receiving my oral direction," he said in a silken drawl.

And...I'd heard enough. I had my own sexual tension to deal with. I didn't need a front row seat to theirs. I stood and mumbled good-bye.

Breck waited for me by the rear exit. "Did you get enough to eat?"

"I guess. Sort of a bizarre dinner conversation so I don't really remember what I ate."

He chuckled. "That's Stirling for you."

Once we were outside, he briefly placed his hand on the small of my back to guide me. "Let's start the tour this way."

Even that single touch caused my stomach to cartwheel.

Blue light glowed from the big top. An electric guitar strummed once. Then twice.

"Sounds like the dance is about to start," Breck said.

"I didn't know there was a dance."

"I don't think it'll go late. Most of the guests left as soon as they finished eating." He walked closer to me. "You ever danced with a guy, Cres?"

"Like gone out two-steppin'? Nah. No clubs that cater to that around here. Gotta go into Denver to find that. What about you?"

"I've hit a gay dance club a time or two. Slow dancin' is easier with a guy because there's no fighting about who's gonna lead."

I smiled. "True. So if you don't mind me asking...how'd you get this job workin' for the Gradskys?"

"Macon Gradsky contacted me. We've stayed in touch over the years." A funny look must've crossed my face because he clarified, "Macon isn't gay. He and I were competitors. We met for the first time at the National High School Rodeo finals. He was the All-Around champ for Colorado and I was All-Around champ for South Dakota." He flashed that megawatt grin. "I whupped his ass in tie-down ropin' and bulldoggin'. He beat me in saddle bronc ridin'. We both ended up attending University of Wyoming and were teammates on the college circuit. I went pro after I graduated and he went to law school."

"Sounds like you've known the Gradsky family for quite a while."

"Rodeo is a small world." He smiled sadly. "A small-minded world too."

"So was it your decision not to go on the podium and introduce yourself tonight? Or did your bosses ask you to hang back?"

"Fully my decision. The focus tonight needed to be on them, not on me." He blocked the path so I couldn't race away. "The Gradskys know you're gay?"

"Kind of a hard secret to keep with London as my sister-in-law." I said dryly. "But yeah, they know."

None of the yard lights were on around the buildings. Probably to keep guests from wandering. A tiny sliver of moon did little to slice through the darkness. I wondered if that darkness made it easier for Breck to take my hand.

My heart jumped into my throat. It'd been so long since I'd had that simple connection it felt foreign.

That's because it's not Mick's hand.

Breck's hand was bigger. Rougher. Stronger from years of handling coarse ropes. He locked his fingers more tightly to mine. Mick's hands had always been cold and clammy—and it bothered him enough that we rarely held hands. Even when we were home alone.

Why are you thinking about that? Every comparison you make will add to your uncertainty. If you can't follow through with simple handholding, let him know now.

Fuck that. I could do this. I *had* to do this.

And I'd take it far beyond handholding.

As soon as we cleared the corner of the next building, I dropped Breck's hand and pushed him against the bricks. "Take off your hat."

He removed his hat with his left hand and let it fall to his side, holding it lightly against his thigh. Automatically his right hand came up and he ran his fingers through his dark hair, trying to get rid of the mark the hat band had left.

It shouldn't have been a sexy move, but with him, it was. Because I knew even when it was dark, Breck retained his pride that he wanted to look good for me.

"Aren't you ditching your hat too?" he asked in a raspy tone.

"Not yet. Keep your right hand by your side too."

"Fuck, Cres, I wanna touch you."

With me standing on the cement curb, we were eye to eye. Mouth to mouth. I flattened my palms beside his head and leaned in until we were groin to groin. "You'll get your chance, just not right now."

A soft grunt escaped him and gusted across my lips when I rocked my pelvis into his.

His cock was already hard.

So was mine.

I pressed my lips to his and held them there. Then I slowly started to move them. A little to the left. A little to the right, keeping up that easy glide until his lips were fuller. Softer. Wetter. I dipped my tongue in the seam, licking the inside edge of his upper lip and then his lower. Getting a taste of him.

Like smoke and whiskey. Not the minty taste I associated with Mick.

That's good. Keep going.

I convinced myself I was anticipating, not stalling. That I was treating this tease as a test to see if Breck could control his dominant nature and let me set the pace.

Are you sure it's not a test for you? To see if you freak out when you remember that the lips clinging to yours aren't Mick's?

Stop.

Breck deserved my full attention.

When I allowed our tongues to touch, he growled, "Fucking kiss me already."

That's all I needed. I dove into his mouth like I owned it.

Greed overwhelmed me.

Yes. *Yes.* This.

Fuck. I needed so much more of *this.*

My head spun as I went at that lush mouth from every angle. My hand cupped his jaw so I could open him up wider, get deeper. Our tongues stroked. Our lips pursed and pressed and glided and teased.

Harsh panting breaths echoed around us and mingled together. Soft groans. The click of teeth. The sounds of passion.

I could not get enough.

I'd missed this urgency. Craved it.

How had I survived without it? It hadn't ever been this way with Mick. Not even in the beginning.

It'd only ever been this way with Breck.

Seemed I'd forgotten that too.

I broke my mouth free, sliding across Breck's smoothly shaven skin to drag my teeth down his jaw, nipping at his chin and the tender flesh of his neck.

Breck let out a muttered, "Christ." Then he tilted his head to the side, giving me full access to his throat, and I nearly snarled with satisfaction. I'd never had his surrender.

Now I did.

Now I wanted it all.

And I'd take it all.

Pushing back on my heels, I reached for his belt buckle, my mouth continuing to maraud his neck and jaw as I unbuttoned and unzipped his jeans. Hooking my fingers inside the waistband beside his hipbones, I tugged his jeans and briefs down to the middle of his thighs.

He hissed in a sharp breath when I lowered to my knees.

I didn't tease. I brought the stiff length into my mouth in a single, greedy gulp.

Then I froze.

That's when the "this is wrong, this isn't Mick" voice became louder.

My thoughts warred with reality. The unfamiliar—yet it was familiar—taste on my tongue. The additional girth stretching my lips. The musky aroma filling my lungs that was all man…but wasn't my man.

My eyes watered.

Not because I wanted to cry.

I gagged.

Not because I didn't want to do this.

I fisted my hand around the base of his shaft and slid my mouth up, my lips catching on the rim of his cockhead. Then I twisted my hand up that meaty cock as I bobbed my head down, hollowing my cheeks with every suctioning pull.

A surprised, "Jesus," exploded above me, followed by a rush of ragged exhales.

Lean hips pumped away from the wall toward my mouth.

Then strong fingers curled around my throat, stopping all motion. His dick slipped free when those fingers latched onto my jaw and tilted my head back.

My gaze collided with Breck's as he squeezed his shaft in the middle, creating a makeshift cock ring. He continued to drag the wet head of his cock across my lips.

"If it hadn't been so long since I had my dick sucked I'd tell you to slow down. But when I'm this close I need to know if I'm coming in your mouth."

I nodded.

"Take your hat off, Cres," he murmured huskily. "Keep your eyes on mine."

A shiver worked through me as I set my Stetson on the ground.

Just like that, he'd taken charge.

Just like that, I'd let him.

For now.

Breck tenderly ran his fingers across my scalp before grabbing a fistful of my hair and directing my head to where he wanted it. His eyes glittered with lust as he began to fuck my mouth, each measured stroke faster and faster until that moment when he shoved in so deep my teeth dug into the root of his cock.

Breck groaned and his dick jerked on my tongue.

Thick bursts of come coated the back of my throat. He didn't have to tell me to suck hard and swallow; I knew exactly what he needed.

That's what I needed too. The heady rush of power. The give and take of control. Of surrender. The suspense of whose will to be on top would win out.

He released my hair and pulled out of my mouth, slumping back against the bricks, eyes squeezed shut, his chest heaving.

In the distance I heard music. In my peripheral vision I saw headlights sweep across the tall grass bordering the fence. Whoops and hollers drifted from someplace.

Resting on my knees in the dark, with my painfully hard dick pressing against the button-fly of my 501s, my jaw sore, I felt entirely disconnected. An overwhelming urge to escape had me blindly reaching for my hat and pushing to my feet.

"Don't run off," Breck said gruffly, when I took a step back off the curb. "I ain't close to done with you tonight." He situated his hat on his head and righted his clothing, never taking his eyes off mine. Then he reached for me. "The tour can wait."

"Okay."

"I can't." Breck loomed over me. "Christ, I want you." He shoved his left hand in the front of my jeans and latched onto me by my belt, his knuckles brushing my erection as he held me in place. He angled his head above mine without banging our hats together—a trick I'd never managed when I locked lips with another cowboy. This kiss was all sweet seduction and gratitude.

My free hand landed on his chest. I was bowled over by his tenderness—something I never expected from a guy who considered fucking an endurance sport.

He murmured, "Come to my place. Even for just a couple of hours."

I slowly licked his lower lip. "If that's what you want."

"Oh, I want all right."

His wicked grin sent my pulse tripping.

We walked hand in hand up the road and cut through the last open area before the tree line. The path grew steeper. By the time we crested the hill, we were both breathing hard again.

That's when I noticed we were in a campground, complete with electrical hookups for each unit space and a private picnic shelter.

"What's this place?" I asked.

"Campground for staff."

"You live in a camper?"

"Yep. The one on the end is mine." Breck stopped in front of a motor home too damn fancy to be called a camper. I'd seen rock star tour buses on TV that were trailer trash compared to this.

"You win the lottery?" Or maybe he'd won a lawsuit. Since he indicated he was buddies with Macon Gradsky, it was a possibility they'd sued the magazine for damages and gone after the CRA for discrimination. From listening to London talk about her brother, Macon was one sue-happy motherfucker.

"This isn't mine from lottery winnings—either from the state or a lawsuit lottery. When I decided to wander, I needed someplace to call home. I bought this with the money I had left." He opened the door and a motorized step popped out. "Go on in."

The inside was ten times more impressive than the outside. I sort of stood there with my mouth hanging open.

A *whoosh* sounded after I watched Breck poke a button that shut the door. The blinds were already down, obstructing the view out the windows. But no one could see in either.

Breck stalked me. "Tell me what you want, Cres."

I stood my ground, even when my heart jackhammered and the first flutters of panic made breathing difficult. Then we were chest to chest, groin to groin. "What are my options?"

He removed my hat and set it on the table next to his. "You want seduction? Rolling around on my bed naked for an hour of foreplay before I fuck you?" He brushed his lips across the top of my ear. "Or should we skip that and I suck you off before I bend you over my table and fuck you?"

"Maybe I want option C. You already got yours; I take mine by bending you over the arm of the couch."

"You are more assertive than you used to be," he murmured in my ear. "I like that. It's hot as hell. Means you're gonna make me work for it. I love a challenge, so let's see where this goes."

I didn't argue as Breck propelled me backward, his mouth plastered to mine, his hands on me everywhere. Making me hard. Making me dizzy.

We stopped when the backs of my knees connected with a solid surface. He broke the kiss and placed his hand on my chest, pushing me until my ass hit the mattress.

"You look good on my bed, Cres."

When Breck leaned over, I grabbed ahold of his shirt and pulled him on top of me. Yeah, he was a big guy, but I wasn't exactly a 98-pound weakling.

Still, the move surprised him.

It really surprised him when I rolled him beneath me and nestled my ass against his groin. Keeping my gaze on his, I said, "Still wanna see the aggressive side of me?"

"Fuck, yeah."

I rocked against the thick length of his erection pressing between my butt cheeks.

Breck groaned and reached for my hips. "Shift back. I wanna feel your cock rubbing on mine."

I laughed softly. "Topping me from below ain't happening."

A devilish gleam entered his eyes. "I already got off once. I just wanted to even things up, but whatever. You're on top."

"Damn straight. Now unbutton your shirt," I said, still grinding against him.

His hands went to his throat and he undid the first button. "You did have a thing for my chest."

"Let's see if I still do. Hurry up."

Once he'd reached the last button above the waist of his jeans, I lifted up so he could untuck his shirt. Then he spread the two sides open, gifting me an unobstructed view of his upper body.

My dick went harder yet and a growl of approval rumbled out.

A thick mat of dark hair furred his chest. He'd lost some of the bulk, but his pectorals were still beautifully defined, as were his abs. The flat brown nipples—almost invisible unless he was aroused—poked up, as if begging for my mouth.

"Jesus, Cres. Stop licking your lips like that. You're gonna make me shoot my load in my damn jeans."

I pressed my thumbs on his nipples, spreading my fingers outward, digging the tips into his sides between his armpits and his ribcage. As I angled forward I had to shift down his lower body so we were nose to nose. "Touch me."

Breck clamped his big mitts onto my butt. He squeezed the flesh and pressed down, adding more pressure to our cocks grinding together. A confident grin tipped up his lips before he fused them to mine. His voracity pulsed through our bodies like a sonic wave each time he sucked on my tongue. My mouth throbbed when he slowed the kiss and tasted the underside of my top and bottom lips with lazy sweeps of his tongue.

That's when the tingling started at the base of my spine.

Too soon. I wasn't ready for this to end. It felt like we'd just started.

"Cres." Breck nudged my chin up and nipped my jawline with firm-lipped bites. "Undo our jeans. Rub your cock against mine. Skin on skin."

I wanted the heat and hardness. The urgency. The musky scent of spunk and sweat.

He knew I was about to give in and he did the one thing that'd guarantee it. He whispered, "Please."

I pushed myself up and scooted back so my knees bracketed the outside of his thighs.

Breck rose up to rest on his elbows, so he could watch me unbuckle and unzip him. His chest was damp, billowing in and out as he rolled his pelvis so I could tug his jeans and briefs down to his shins. My knuckles smacked into the top of his boot shaft, startling me. We'd been so crazed for each other we hadn't taken off our boots.

Time to rectify that.

I hopped off the bed.

His right eyebrow winged up. "Goin' someplace?"

I grabbed the heel of his right boot and lifted, yanking it off his foot. Repeated it on the left side.

Grinning, I pantsed him.

Then I undid my belt and unzipped before I crawled back between his legs.

His smile faded. "Why am I mostly naked and you're not?"

I flattened my palms by his head, keeping my body in a pushup position over his as I brushed my lips over the divot in his chin. "I want you feelin' the friction from the denim scraping the inside of your thighs as I'm grinding on you." My lips traveled up to his ear. "I want you to hear the buckle on my belt clanking as I'm moving above you." I sank my teeth into his earlobe and he arched up. "I want you to remember this. I don't want to be another anonymous quickie fuck, Breck."

Where the hell had that come from? I sounded possessive and commanding. As if I expected this to be more than a one-time blowjob and rub off.

"You never were that, Cres, even when that's all you were supposed to be." Breck jerked my jeans and boxer briefs down to the middle of my thighs. He followed the crease of my ass up, ending at my lower back.

When he reached between us and his knuckles grazed my balls, I started like a frightened rabbit. It'd been a lifetime since any hand beside my own had touched my cock.

He stroked me and stared into my face, his fierce eyes issuing a challenge. "You sure you don't wanna straddle my face so I can suck you off?"

"Still topping from below." I lowered my pelvis, forcing him to let go of my dick. I hissed in a breath when our cocks touched and adjusted my hips so the rim of his cockhead caught on mine with every upstroke.

"Oh, fuck. That's…" He groaned as I rubbed my rigid shaft over the sweet spot below the head of his cock.

"Still want me to stop and fuck your mouth?" I whispered against his temple.

"No. Goddamn you're good at this. Don't ever fucking stop." His fingers dug into my ass and he tilted his head to conquer my mouth in a sizzling kiss.

That dizzying sense of urgency assailed me and I began to move with more enthusiasm than finesse.

Wet mouths, hot, hard, damp bodies in motion. The heated scent of his skin, the addicting taste of his mouth proved to be too much and I teetered on the edge.

He pumped his hips, his body shaking beneath mine. "I need it faster."

"Do it."

Clamping his big fist around both of our dicks, he jerked us off. "Fuck. Yes."

I started to come, his name on my lips as I shot my load in hot bursts of ass clenching pleasure.

His sexy grunts of satisfaction followed.

After my cock quit twitching and the buzzing in my head faded, I collapsed on top of him. Burying my face in the crook of his neck, my lips searching for the spot on his throat where his pulse always jumped wildly.

But it wasn't there, next to his voice box.

I murmured, "That was a nice change of pace."

The body below mine shook with humor. "Nice? That was fucking spectacular."

I froze.

Not Mick's voice—he never swore.

I inhaled.

Not Mick's scent—he always wore cologne.

And because I was either losing my mind or a fucking masochist, when I licked the skin beneath my lips, it wasn't the clean taste of Mick's sweat. This was earthier. More…primal.

I scrambled upright so fast my cock jerked free from the hand surrounding it with enough force my balls stung from the sharp pain.

Then I was staring into slumberous blue eyes, not brown.

The smile on the full red lips was decidedly cocky, not sweet.

Holy fuck.

Since Breck wore that sated look…maybe he hadn't heard me saying another man's name when I spurted all over his hand.

Shame burned through me.

I was off the bed and fastening my jeans and belt before Breck knew anything was wrong.

So very wrong.

"Cres? What's goin' on?"

"I can't do this. I'm sorry. I've gotta go."

"What? Jesus. Just wait a damn minute."

But I didn't.

I ran out like a fucking coward.

Chapter Four

Breck

The next morning I went looking for Sutton Grant.

Most of the staff had stayed over after the party last night. And I knew from Berlin's complaints that London wasn't an early riser so chances were good they were still around.

The tricky part would be asking Sutton what was wrong with his brother without rousing his suspicions. I wasn't sure Cres would appreciate being linked to me given the fact he'd run out on me.

Chapped my ass every time I thought about it.

The construction workers had already disassembled the biggest tent and were packing up chairs. I cut across the road to the cafeteria.

Sure enough, Sutton held court by the buffet.

I sauntered over to the industrial coffee urn and filled a cup.

The guys wrapped up their conversation as soon as I approached them. The paranoia still lingered that people were talking about me when a discussion abruptly ended if I was within earshot.

"Morning," I said to Sutton.

"Hey, Breck." He pointed with his chin to my cup of coffee. "Fair warning that London made the coffee. It's got a serious kick."

I looked around for her. "Where is your better half?"

"Helping Grandma Berlin fill my truck with more shit for Brennen. I swear we could open a damn toy store with all the stuff both sets of his grandparents buy him."

"You're not really complaining, buddy."

Sutton smiled. "Only when I have to haul it and set it up. But the look on my boy's face is worth it." He paused. "What's goin' on with you?"

"Just wandering around. It appears the open house was a success."

"Thank God it's over. Now I'll get my wife back. She's been stayin' here three nights a week getting ready for it."

"Shame she's not teachin'." I hid my smirk behind my cup.

"Bite your damn tongue," he shot back. "The woman's temperament is better suited to workin' with horses than people."

"Looked like London was tearin' it up last night."

"Cres's fault. He started her on the tequila."

There was the angle I needed. "So Cres didn't stick around last night?"

"He drove Wyn's truck home since he had to feed cattle this morning. Why?"

"He forgot to give me his number last night after"—*he came all over my hand and took off like his ass was on fire*—"we spent time talkin' and stuff. Wondered if you'd give it to me."

Sutton's eyes narrowed. "I saw you two *talkin'*."

"You say that like we were doin' something besides talkin'," I said evenly.

"Were you? You both disappeared for a while."

"Not exactly what I asked. Not any of your business either."

"Along those same lines, if he'd wanted you to have his number, he would've given it to you, doncha think?" Sutton retorted.

That was a little hard to do when he had my cock in his mouth. "Look. If you don't want to give it to me, that's cool." *I'll just get it from someone else* went unsaid.

Sutton studied me before he sighed. "I'm protective of him."

"Why? I get that he's your younger brother, but he is an adult."

"Cres has had a rough go of it and I don't want you takin' advantage of him." Sutton's gaze hardened. "Like you did a few years ago when I sent him to you to deal with my horse."

"Cres was an adult then too. He made his own choices. And fuck you if you think his bein' with me back then somehow turned him gay."

"Whoa. I never said that and I sure as hell didn't mean to imply it." He paused. "Let's start over. This isn't meant to be accusatory. But when you were talkin' with Cres last night, did you tell him about bein' outed and all the crap that happened afterward?"

"Yeah. I always thought you were bein' humble when you said not everyone in your family rabidly followed rodeo." I sipped my coffee. "He didn't know anything about it."

"Not surprised. People outside the world of rodeo would likely shrug and wonder why it'd been such a big deal." He folded his arms on his chest. "So part of me wonders why you'd willingly put yourself back into this world, Breck."

My cheeks heated. "It's not like I have another skill set. And besides, don't think I don't know that *you're* the one who suggested me as a possible instructor for the Gradskys' rodeo school. Macon made the call, but that happened at your urging, Sutton."

He grinned. "I figured if they couldn't have me, they'd want the second best champion bulldogger...which is you."

"You're hilarious. And if I haven't said it, I appreciate your faith in me." Before things got sappy or awkward, I added, "So why didn't you take the job? Since your wife is here all the time anyway?"

"After I survived that last run, during my stint in the hospital I swore that I was done throwing myself off the back of a galloping horse onto a steer. It's a promise I've kept."

"Bein' a teacher doesn't mean you have to actually demonstrate," I pointed out.

"Maybe not for you and the way you teach, but it does for me. I've told my in-laws I'll fill in if the need arises." Sutton gave me another shit-eating grin. "So if you want a *four*-time world champion bulldogger as a guest lecturer, I'd be happy to swing by your classroom."

"Don't be surprised if it ends up bein' permanent for you. The students—or their parents—might run me out on a rail anyway."

Sutton shook his head. "Ain't gonna happen. Chuck and Berlin will stand behind you, Breck. Whether you have a chick or a dude in your bed at the end of the night has no bearing on your past credentials and shouldn't be allowed to diminish your expertise."

"Thanks."

"No problem. And I'll go you one better than giving you Cres's phone number. I'll give you his address so you can drop off the pneumatic drill I borrowed from him. I've got too much baby junk in my truck."

I'd take any excuse to talk to Cres and find out what had happened last night.

"I'll drive over to your campsite and drop it off. Say…fifteen minutes?"

"Sounds good."

I was leaning against my Jeep when Sutton pulled up. The pneumatic drill wasn't big, so I recognized his excuse of not having enough room in his 350 diesel truck was total horseshit. I tried not to dissect why Sutton had changed his mind about me corrupting his younger brother.

He handed me a scrap of paper. "Here's Cres's address for you to punch into the GPS." He slammed the hatchback door on the Jeep. "Like I said before, Cres had a rough go the last two years so I'm glad to see him…" He sighed. "Sounds clichéd to say livin' again, but it's true."

"What's been goin' on with him?"

Sutton's head snapped up so fast his hat nearly tumbled off his head. "He didn't tell you about Mick?"

A bad feeling rolled over me. "Not a word."

"You really didn't do a lot of talkin', did you?" He held up his hand. "Sorry. None of my business."

"We talked a lot, Sutton. Just not about Mick." I'd asked Cres what he'd been up to and he'd hedged. Even when I'd called him on it, he'd managed to sidestep any conversation about his life. And I'd let him.

"That little shit. I'm gonna wring his damn neck."

"Who's Mick? An ex or something?"

"Mick was his boyfriend. They met at our wedding and moved in together. Two years ago Mick was killed in a freak accident. Cres shut down after that. And I hate to admit this, but Wyn and Mel had a baby a few months before Mick died, and then me and London had Brennen. We were busy with our lives and didn't butt into his. Last night was the first time we forced him into a social situation that wasn't only our immediate family. And he wouldn't have come if we'd given him any advance notice or if Wyn hadn't driven him."

Now Cres running out on me made sense. It also gave me an odd feeling of loss—like I'd already lost Cres because he belonged to someone else. "I'm glad you forced his appearance."

"And now I'm forcing yours." He glanced over his shoulder. "Good thing Wyn didn't notice you and Cres talkin'."

"Why?"

"Wyn ain't your biggest fan. He'd discourage…hell he'd probably campaign to keep Cres from spending time with you."

I frowned. "I'm confused. I don't know Wyn. I've met him like once."

"But he thinks he knows you. Do you even remember bein' a total prick to Mel at our wedding?"

I shook my head. "I barely remember bein' at your wedding. My date drove; I drank and ended up passing out in the motel room. I woke up to discover she'd snuck out at some point during the night with all of my cash." I felt the heat of shame spread across my face and neck. "I understand why Wyn would have a problem with me if I acted like a drunken fucktard."

"Pretty much," he said with far too much glee.

"Does Mel feel the same way about me?"

"I don't know. You always were a cocky, manipulative, condescending asshat. I know you've changed. London and her family have embraced the changes you've made. They've accepted the man you are now. As far as anyone else…including my brother? You'd better brush up on the charm that used to come so naturally."

"Awesome."

He clapped me on the shoulder. "Good luck."

* * * *

I pulled up to Cres's place around lunchtime. He lived in a log house— not the norm in Eastern Colorado. Off to the left side by the garage stood a row of evergreens. On the right side was a corral and a metal barn. I gave the rest of the area a passing look after Cres ambled out of the house and paused at the top of the steps on the front porch.

Immediately after I climbed out of my rig, a dog tore out of the barn, snapping and snarling as it barreled toward me.

Cres bounded down the steps, yelling, "Banjo, knock it off."

By the time the Australian shepherd skidded to a stop by head-butting my knees, he'd lowered his hackles and was wagging his tail. I crouched down to pet him. "Banjo, huh? Bud, I'm afraid your bark is worse than your bite."

Banjo yipped and tried to lick my face.

I grinned and let him. I missed having a dog.

"Banjo, go lay down," Cres commanded.

The dog circled me one more time before he trotted up the porch steps and out of sight.

I stood and propped my hands on my hips. Let him take the first stab at conversation.

He said, "Let me guess. You were just in the neighborhood."

"It's a hard place to find without GPS."

"It's an even harder place to find when my name, address, and phone number are unlisted."

"Sutton asked me to return your pneumatic drill. Blame him for breaching your privacy. But he refused to give me your cell phone number, so it's kind of a wash." I paused. "Then again, he did tell me about Mick. So you might want to chew his ass about that."

His posture stiffened. "What'd he say about him?"

"More than you did, that's for damn sure. So I'm here because I wanna hear it from you, Cres. I'll even tell you where I want you to start. Back to our conversation last night when I asked what you'd been up to and all you said was ranching with Wyn."

Cres turned and focused on a spot beyond the horizon, giving me his profile. The muscle in his jaw bunched and I could almost hear him grinding his teeth together.

Seemed like an hour passed, but when I glanced at my watch, it'd only been five minutes. Still, that was a long time to exist in silence.

You don't need this. Sure, you like Cres. Maybe you've always liked him a little too much. But right now, he's a former hookup. That's all he sees you as. Take the hint and move on.

Cres remained in the "stare at nothing" state when I took the drill out of the back of my truck and carried it to the porch.

I paused behind him and said, "Take care." I'd almost made it to the sanctity of my truck when Cres spoke.

"I loved Mick. We were inseparable almost from the moment we met. He died just over two years ago when a car slipped off its jack and crushed him."

An ugly death. Accidents left survivors with too many "what if" scenarios and guilt the accident could've been prevented. I ached for him.

"When you told me that you lost everything after you were outed on the circuit, my first thought was…you don't really know what it's like to lose everything."

The anger in his tone? Not a surprise. The derision? Unnecessary and unfair. I faced him. "Death trumps everything. Got it. Sorry that I burdened you with my insignificant life problems. Don't worry. You're still the champ in the 'shittiest life event' contest that I didn't realize we were playing." I stepped closer to the driver's side door. "Sorry for your loss, Cres."

"Don't go."

I paused with my boot on the running board.

"I know I sound like a dick. But I didn't get to finish that train of thought before you jumped in," Cres said testily.

"I'm listening."

"For a year and a half, I believed I'd lost everything when Mick died. It's just been in the past few months that I could face the truth. *I* gave up everything as a result of Mick's death. He's the only thing I lost. But I can't go back and I've been fucking petrified to try to go forward. I haven't talked to anyone about it."

That admission smoothed the rough edges of my anger.

"Seein' you last night...was the first time I felt like movin' on." Cres jammed his hand through his hair. "Trauma, grief, whatever is not a competition. I'm sorry if it sounded like I one-upped you."

"Why didn't you tell me about Mick last night?"

His head snapped up. "Because I wanted to see if I could be a normal single guy again. Acting on an attraction to a hot guy who knew nothin' about what I'd been through."

"And?"

"And you were there. I fucking ran out on you when it got to be too much."

"You also gave me one helluva blowjob. You almost had me coming in my jeans before you stripped them off and made me come again." I locked my gaze to his. "From where I'm standing, you had no problem acting on your attraction to me."

Cres broke eye contact. "I said his name."

"What?"

"When I started to come, I said Mick." His gaze returned to my face. "That's why I ran out."

"And you thought I'd what? Knock you on your ass if you told me that?"

He erased the distance between us and got right in my face. "Why the hell are you bein' so reasonable about this, Breck?"

I have no fucking idea.

I fisted my hand in his shirt and hauled him closer. "Because I want more of you, dumbass. A whole lot more." My mouth crashed down on his and I kissed the shit out of him. He had an aggressive streak, but it was nothing compared to mine. Nothing.

He wasn't the only one who'd had a recent revelation. I'd stared at the damn ceiling for three fucking hours after he'd left last night. Not only wondering what had happened to make him run, but wondering when I'd lost my goddamned balls and hadn't chased after him. When had I turned into the mild-mannered gentleman cowboy who hid in his motor home? I'd always been the guy who went after what he wanted—men, women, championships, sponsorships. I'd let the system, a goddamned system that failed me, dictate the kind of man I became after I'd risen from the ashes of my spectacular crash and burn.

No. More.

Cres eased up on the kiss. He kept one hand twined in my hair and the other hand flattened on my chest. "Sorry I fucked up and didn't tell you about Mick."

"I'm not the same asshole guy I used to be."

"You never were an asshole to me, Breck."

There was that sweetness again.

Cres confessed, "I'm still a little screwed up."

"Aren't we all screwed up about something?"

"I guess." He sighed. "I gotta admit, this isn't goin' like I envisioned when I saw your Jeep pull up. But I am really glad you chased me down."

"I should've done it last night. But bein's I was buck-ass nekkid and you weren't, you had a head start." I slid my hand beneath his jawbone and feathered my thumb across his bottom lip. "It turns me the fuck on when your lips get like this, full and red and shiny. I could get used to seein' them like that all the time."

Cres's body went taut.

Even when I had good intentions, I somehow messed up by saying or doing the wrong thing. "What's wrong?"

"Just because I said I was testing the waters to see if I'm ready to move on, I'm not lookin' for a relationship ever again."

"Never?"

"Love ain't worth the trouble of the heartache you get when you lose it."

I should've run then. Instead, I shrugged as if my heart wasn't hurting for him. And hurting for myself since I'd never been lucky enough to have that kind of love. "I'm not here for the long haul anyway."

His gaze turned shrewd. "How long are you here?"

"For the first session, which is nine weeks. Then I'll decide if I'm cut out for teachin'. But I'll warn ya, I've still got itchy feet even after spending twenty years livin' on the road. I like it. It's part of who I am so I don't see that changing any time soon."

"What are you saying?" he asked.

"We'll be in the same area for nine weeks. We could have a lot of fun together exploring this. If it gets boring, we'll end it, no harm, no foul." That wasn't entirely true. I'd pull out all the stops to ensure we'd spend every free moment of those nine weeks together.

"Just fucking? No relationship?"

I continued to stroke his lip as my gaze wandered over his face. "Even if we're just fucking, Cres, we *are* in a relationship. That can be whatever we want it to outside of the hot sex. My days of sharing are over." I figured it'd be hard enough sharing him with the ghost of Mick.

He tried to drop his chin to hide his eyes, but that was bullshit.

I forced him to meet my gaze. "No more half-truths or secrets. Talk to me. Even if you think it'll piss me off."

"I haven't been with anyone since Mick," he blurted out. "That's the other reason I ran out. I wasn't sure how far I could go."

"Guess we'll see if I can convince you to go all the way with me." I grinned. "It wasn't too difficult that week you came to Denver…I had your cock in my mouth within two hours of us meeting. I had you bent over with my cock in your ass that same night."

He groaned. "Smartass. Be serious. This could be a problem."

"If we get to a point that you're freakin' out, tell me. I ain't gonna get mad or jealous about Mick. I don't have a right to it. But I ain't gonna lie. I want the rights to this." I reached down and palmed his hard-on, letting my fingers slide back and rub his balls. "If I had my way? I'd blow you right here against the side of my Jeep to remind you how good it is between us."

His cock jumped beneath my palm and his eyes burned hot.

Interesting.

"What ranch chores you doin' this afternoon?"

"Nothin' pressing this week. Why?"

"I thought I'd give you the tour of Grade A Rodeo Academy if you weren't busy later. Then I could fix us supper and we could hang out for a while tonight."

Cres's eyes narrowed. "You cook?"

"I'm a thirty-eight-year-old bachelor. Of course I cook." I leaned in and dragged my lips across his ever so slightly. "We did more than fuck and suck that week in Denver."

"Then why did you bail on me? I showed up that last morning and you'd already gone."

It'd sound like I was pandering if I told him our connection had spooked me because it'd happened so fast. Cres deserved more than the man I'd been at that time of my life—secretive and on a path of self-destruction. Being my usual dickish self, I'd left him first before he could leave me. "I'm not tryin' to charm my way into your jeans when I say I thought about you a lot over that next year."

"Same here. I intended to talk to you at Sutton and London's wedding. I'd heard you were on a destructive path and when I saw firsthand how bitter and angry you'd gotten, I thought maybe I could get through to you. But then…"

"Then you met Mick."

"Yeah."

"Was it lust at first sight?"

"He was buff as fuck, so that part of the attraction was a no-brainer. But he worked with Sutton and I hadn't been out long enough to know if it was…" He scratched his chin. "Acceptable, I guess…to go after a guy if I wasn't sure that he preferred sucking a prick to eating a pussy."

I laughed. "Crude. So how'd you figure out he was a dick-smoker?"

Cres held his fist up for a bump. "Equally crude. And if I would've said that to Mick? He would've blushed and stammered. For bein' former military, he had few vices."

"Besides lovin' the D," I said slyly.

"Yeah. Anyway I think we were at a community barbecue and we got to talkin'. He asked me out for coffee. We had a few dates. I hadn't been too sure about him in the beginning since he didn't have much experience. But he was eager. And the more I got to know him, the more I realized Mick was just one of those genuinely good guys. Honest, brave, and true. Helpful, loyal, obedient."

I didn't point out it sounded like he was describing a dog.

"He stuck around after my dad had his heart attack. He helped Mel when she had issues with her diabetes. His sweet nature appealed to me, you know? Then after the first time we fucked, he moved in." Cres blinked. "Shit. Sorry. Didn't mean to go off on a mangent."

"Mangent?"

"When you don't shut up about the guy in your life."

I chuckled. "Never heard that one before."

He smirked. "Because you're old."

"Hilarious. Guess I'll toddle off to the old folk's home, sonny boy, and drink my Metamucil before *Wheel of Fortune* comes on."

Cres laughed. I liked to hear it because I suspected there hadn't been much humor in his life in recent years.

I fished my phone out of my back pocket. "Hit me with your number." As soon as I had the info saved, I sent him a text. "Now you have mine."

"Good. I'll be there about three."

"That'll work. Text me if anything changes."

Chapter Five

Breck

Patience—a trait I'd never had much use for.

Practicing restraint? Not a natural reaction for me either.

But I had no choice but to implement both from the moment Cres had shown up for his personal tour of Grade A Rodeo Academy.

When I'd shown him the empty classrooms I'd exercised restraint, even when my brain kept replaying the image of me on my knees between Cres's legs, my head bobbing as I noisily sucked him off as he braced himself against my desk.

I filed that away as a future possibility. That counted as patience, right?

Hour two into the tour, after I'd introduced him to the other instructors as Sutton's brother and we'd chatted with Berlin and Chuck Gradsky, I decided I deserved a fucking medal for patience, restraint, and circumspection for not dragging his sexy ass into the boiler room and fingering his prostate until he jizzed all over my chest.

Yeah, that scenario would shock the stuffing out of Bill, the groundskeeper. But I'd put a note in the suggestion box that maybe the boiler room door needed a proper lock.

I was getting the hang of this "being a team player" shit.

By hour three—Cres's patience had worn thin.

And that tested the fuck out of my restraint because we were near the end of the tour.

In the first arena, he'd grabbed me by the shirt and kissed the sense out of me.

I'd kissed him back because I sure as hell wasn't shooting for sainthood.

In the second arena, he'd stood behind me and started rubbing his groin into my ass, suggesting a hand job to relax me.

My cock had pouted when I resisted the temptation.

In the third arena, Cres warned me if I didn't end the tour in the next seconds he was going home.

It might've been the only time in my life I gave in to an ultimatum with zero resentment.

He asked, "How far is the campground from here?"

"A ten-minute walk." Or a four-minute run.

Then again, running with a hard-on sucked.

When my motor home came into view, I clicked the key fob that unlocked and opened the door.

My eyes were on his butt as he jogged up the steps.

As soon as my boot hit the top step, Cres was on me, his mouth ravenous, his fingers at the hollow of my throat as he undid all of the pearl-snap buttons on my shirt with one vicious tug.

I circled my hand beneath his jaw, breaking free from that tempting mouth so I could think. "Hey, horny toad, how about you let me close the door before you tear off my clothes?"

"Then hurry the fuck up. You've been shaking that tight cowboy ass at me the last three hours and I want it now."

I shut and locked the door and darkened the blinds, while Cres attacked my neck.

He peeled my shirt down my arms, carelessly tossing it to the floor. He groaned with frustration. "Why are you wearin' another shirt?"

"I always wear an undershirt."

"Next time don't. I hate havin' to strip another layer off you to get to the good stuff."

In the back of my mind I wished I could take the time to bask in Cres's lust for me. I couldn't remember the last time I'd been wanted with such near desperation.

Then he hooked his fingers in my belt loops and towed me down the hallway to my bedroom so fast we nearly tripped.

He laughed. "Keep up."

Normally I'd be the one urging us to get naked as I assumed the dominant role.

So it was a fucking rush to let go and follow Cres's lead.

Once we cleared the doorway to my bedroom, Cres shoved me against the wall and held my arms by my sides, plastering his body to mine. His lips grazed my ear. "Fast and dirty, Breck. That's how I'm gonna fuck you."

"Whatever you want."

He pushed back and dropped his ass to the mattress, keeping his molten gaze on mine as he grabbed the heel of his right cowboy book and yanked it off. A smirk curled his lips when he tipped the boot upside down and two strips of condoms fell on the bed.

I laughed. "Interesting place to keep them."

"Too many to keep in my wallet. Didn't want to run out." He lifted his left foot.

"Got lube in that one?"

Cres tugged his boot off and tipped it on the bed. Individual packets of lube landed on top of the condoms.

I laughed again.

Then Cres was back on his feet. The hunger in his touch, in his eyes, undeniable.

He rid me of the pesky T-shirt. He braced one hand beside my head. "Take off your boots."

Damn difficult to do with his lips leaving wet trails across my collarbones, but I persevered.

He went into full-on attack mode after the first touch of his tongue to my nipple.

My head *thunked* against the wall. The hours working out were worth it to get this reaction out of him. He kept at it, rubbing his face in my chest hair, licking and sucking my nipples, biting them, turning me inside out.

He dropped to his knees and had my jeans around my ankles and my cock in his mouth while I still reeled from his expert nipple play.

I glanced down and cupped his gorgeous face in my palms. "You look really fuckin' hot with my cock in your throat. But I don't wanna come in your mouth, Cres. I wanna come with your cock in my ass." There was power in admitting that I wanted to let go of the fierce control I maintained in every aspect of my life—especially sex—and I trusted him to give me what I needed. Keeping a tight grip on his head, I pushed him back, letting my dick slip out so just the tip rested on his lower lip. Then I thrust in deep, fucking his mouth with fast, confident strokes so he understood that while I had no issue with him fucking me, I'd *never* be a fucking bottom.

When I released him, he said, "Get on the bed. Hands and knees."

I brushed the condoms aside and looked over my shoulder to see him striding forward, buck-ass nekkid.

Whoa. Fifteen seconds ago he'd been fully dressed.

And I saw no sign of the playful man who'd dragged me into my own bedroom. I saw a primal male, oozing raw sexuality and pulsing with conquering greed.

Holy hell. I nearly nutted right then.

Cres rolled the condom on and stroked himself. "Face forward and move your knees closer together."

The bed jiggled as he climbed on.

Immediately he caged me beneath his body—something I wouldn't have believed possible since I had more height and breadth. He nested his cock into the crack of my ass and peppered hot kisses from my left shoulder to my right. Then his lips found my ear and he taunted, "Fast and dirty."

Christ. I was already dangling on the edge and he'd barely touched me.

His tongue followed the line of my spine down.

And down.

And down.

And surely he wasn't going there.

Please, please be going there.

Then his hands were spreading my ass cheeks and his tongue lapped at my hole.

Oh fuck oh fuck oh fuck.

Don't come yet, don't come yet, or he'll stop.

I could hold off if he didn't…and then he did.

Cres gently sucked on the ring of muscles and alternated between soft kisses and tender licks on the clenching pucker. His grunting growls of pleasure vibrated across my skin, sending tingles straight up my spine and down to my balls. His fingertips dug into the globes of my ass with enough pressure to leave bruises.

I'd never wanted the marks of a man's possession as much as I needed his.

Then he plunged his tongue into my ass.

The edges of my consciousness went a little hazy.

Cres must've sensed I couldn't take much more before I'd blow, so he backed off.

I felt a cool smear of lube and the slow press of one finger inside me. I groaned and pushed back, signaling I was ready for more.

He added more lube and another finger, his breath hot in my ear as he prepared me with the patience and surety that kicked my anticipation even higher.

Then the head of his cock rested against my hole.

He didn't ask if I was ready. One hard snap of his hips and his cock was fully embedded in my ass.

My dick slapped against my belly from the driving force when he started to fuck me.

It'd been a dry spell the last year and I should've been wincing in pain. But he'd prepared me well enough that all I felt was the sweet ache of pleasure.

"Gonna have to jack yourself this go," he panted. "Because fuck...I'm almost done in."

I had a moment to bask in the sense of satisfaction that he already teetered on the brink of unraveling—that he'd needed this as much, or maybe more than I did. Balancing on my forearm, I fisted my cock, too far gone to do anything but watch my hand between my legs as I beat off.

I had a zip of warning before my balls tightened and I was spurting into my fist.

Cres grunted and stopped moving completely. The rhythmic squeezing of my anal passage was intense enough to pull his orgasm from him, and he shuddered above me.

Fuck, yeah. That's what I needed.

As I attempted to level my breathing, I snagged the undershirt I'd left on the bed and wiped my sticky hand.

That's when I heard it. An odd-sounding, wounded noise.

A panicked noise.

No fucking way. He wasn't running out on me again. We'd deal with his guilt or sadness or whatever together.

When he started to pull out, to pull back, to pull away, I reached around and clamped my hand behind his quivering thigh. "Don't," I said gruffly. "I need a sec."

That brought him out of it. "Sure. Sorry."

I slowly pushed up onto my knees, keeping his cock—which hadn't seemed to have softened at all—lodged in my ass.

Immediately Cres slid his hands up the front of my body, over my abs, ribs, and chest. He curled his fingers over my shoulders, flattening his palms to my collarbones. He pressed his lips to the nape of my neck and squeezed me tight.

A funny tickle started in my chest and I closed my eyes. Although he had the dominant position, I knew I was holding him up.

Neither of us spoke. Cres clung to me and I continued to hold onto his thigh, letting my thumb sweep across the curve of his ass.

Finally he heaved a huge sigh. "Thanks, man."

"You okay?"

Another sigh. "I am now. It's just…different." His lips whispered across my skin. "That was fuckin' awesome."

I grinned and turned my head to kiss his knuckles. "For me too, buddy."

"I didn't think of him," he confessed. "I was one hundred percent in the moment with you, Breck. I want to make sure you know that."

"You feel guilty about that, Cres?"

"No. And then I felt guilty for not feelin' guilty." He paused. "That's kinda fucked up, isn't it."

I didn't answer because he just needed to say what he was thinking out loud. What a huge feeling of relief that he trusted that I could handle his honesty.

"Thanks for stayin' with me during my little freak-out," he murmured against the slope of my shoulder.

"Well, to be honest, it was a selfish reaction. Because I don't think my ego could've handed it if you would've run out on me twice after we fucked around."

Cres chuckled.

"You wanna get your cock outta my ass now?"

"Not really." He sank his teeth into the spot on the back of my neck that made me goddamned weak in the knees.

Another chuckle vibrated across my back when I swayed against him.

I slapped his ass cheek.

"Okay. I'm goin'. But don't go anywhere."

I turned my head to look him in the eyes. "There's nowhere I'd rather be."

He kissed me with sweetness and surety and passion.

That's when I knew I was already in over my head with this man.

* * * *

Cres insisted we climb under the covers after he dealt with the condom.

My body temp ran hot, so I welcomed the coolness of the sheets as I stretched out on my stomach. I knocked the pillows aside and folded my arms above my head, resting the side of my face on my right biceps, still floating on that post-orgasmic high.

Snuggly Cres wormed his way right next to me. Then his hands were all over me.

Somehow I'd forgotten how damn handsy the guy was after fucking.

He planted a kiss on the ball of my shoulder, his lips soft and sweet.

For the longest time, he was content to drag the tips of his fingers up and down my spine while he rested his cheek on the back of my left arm, his leg hooked over mine. So when his fingers ventured outward and connected with the scar, every bit of my relaxation vanished.

"What's this?"

"A scar."

"No kiddin'. A scar from what?"

"Someone figured they needed to teach me a lesson with a whip." Why had I blurted that out? I should've given him some bullshit lie about a rodeo injury.

"It feels new." His fingers connected with the raised edges of the two scars below it. "How many of these do you have?"

"Not sure," I lied. "It's hard to look at my own back."

"Do you get distracted by your hot ass? Because I sure would."

"You've already had my hot ass. I'll need recovery time before you have it again."

"While I'm waiting, I'll check out these painful-lookin' marks, tough guy." Cres used the remote and cranked up the bedroom lights to full power, searing my retinas. I turned my head toward the wall to block out the light.

Right. That's why you're avoiding eye contact.

The heat of his breath flowed across my skin as he inspected every inch of my back. Every time he found a new mark, he counted it out loud.

I already knew I had twelve visible scars from that night.

Cres had found every one.

The mental scars…there were far more of them.

"How—where—did you get these?"

"They were a belated parting gift from a few guys on the circuit."

"Jesus." Cres swept his hand down my spine and back up. "You didn't consent to this."

"Who the fuck would consent to bein' trussed up half-nekkid while some drunken dude whipped you hard enough to break the skin?" I snapped.

Soothingly he said, "Tell me."

"How about we don't go here because it's one of the most humiliating things that I've been through." Yeah, that'll get him to drop it.

Then sweet Cres vanished. "I don't give a shit. I wanna know how the fuck this happened to you. And I'm as tenacious as a damn bulldog, so start talking."

I'd never told anyone this. I'd just dealt with it and then blocked it out. "After everything went down, and I had no place to go, I bought this motor home. I wandered the country, traveling the back roads."

"No one knew you'd joined the 'go RVing' movement?"

I snorted. "Nope. Although this is a nice ride, it doesn't stand out when you're tooling down the highway or parked at a campground with 200 other motor homes. Paying cash for camping meant I didn't have to register at any of the sites. For all intents and purposes, I disappeared."

"You didn't tell anyone your plans?"

"No one to tell, Cres."

"That sucks." He nuzzled the nape of my neck. "Were you lonely during your journey to the center of nowhere?"

"Solitude forced me to examine aspects of my life that'd been long overdue. I stayed in contact with a few people I trusted, like the Gradskys. I shut down all my social media. But because I'm also a creature of habit, I went to Vegas."

"During finals?" he said sharply.

"Yeah."

"Why the hell did you even care?"

"I went because I'd bought tickets and prepaid my hotel room a year in advance. When I didn't dress like a cowboy or act like king of the damn rodeo, I wasn't on anyone's radar. I'd had two days of anonymous in the stands. On the third day—night—whatever, I hit this dive diner that's off the strip. I sat up at the counter like I always did. Again, nothin' about me said cowboy."

I felt him smile against my skin as he pinched my ass. "Hate to break it to you, dude, but everything about you screams cowboy. Even when you're nekkid. But go on."

"So this hot young guy, probably your age, sits two chairs away and strikes up a conversation with me."

"You didn't think that was suspicious?"

"Nope. Bullshitting with strangers about random stuff is the hallmark of this diner. We kept talkin' even after our food arrived and he moved over to the seat next to mine. Just from the way he looked at me, I knew he was interested. And I hadn't gotten laid for six fucking months. I suggested we hook up and he immediately said yes."

As I struggled to get through this next part, Cres waited, keeping up those tender touches I could easily get addicted to.

"I followed this guy outside and around the back of the building and found myself in a blanket party."

My heart thundered remembering the scratchy wool saddle blanket being pulled over my head. The absolute darkness. The lack of air. The ball-shrinking fear I was about to pay the ultimate price for wanting a few hours of companionship and someone to touch me. "When they started to drag me to the empty field behind the restaurant, I fought back with everything I had."

"Do you know how many guys were involved?"

"Around ten. Took every one of those fuckers to take me down." Stupid point of pride for me, but there it was. I forced myself to take a deep breath. "Even with the blanket over my head I recognized a few of the voices as guys I'd known on the circuit. Some of the shit they said to me...they were seriously sick motherfuckers. I didn't hear it all because they had the blanket around my neck too tight and I passed out. That part wasn't intentional because when I came to, they were arguing about not accidently killin' me. Before I felt any relief I wasn't about to die, they cut my shirt off, tied my wrists together in front of me and draped my arms over a fence post. I made the mistake of tryin' to get free and ended up slicing the shit out of my forearm on the barbed wire. So I knew whatever they'd planned to do to me, I'd just have to stand there and fucking take it." I flinched even now when I recalled the whistling sound of the bullwhip right before the loud crack of leather connecting with my flesh.

"Breck," he breathed in my ear. "You're safe here with me. You don't have to talk about it if you can't."

"I've never told anyone about this, Cres. So just…give me a second."

"Sure. Take your time. I ain't goin' anywhere."

Out of sheer mortification, I continued to face away from him. "One guy laid into me with the whip while his drunken cohorts laid into me about my perversions and bein' an embarrassment to all decent rodeo cowboys. One dickhead called the open gashes a 'bloodletting.' Assholes laughed like fuckin' donkeys about that. Another asswipe said our ancestors had it right. A sicko with my predilection would've been strung up as a warning to others."

"These are the same ancestors that thought slavery was A-Okay," he sneered.

"Right. Then they yanked me from the fence post and tossed me on the ground." Bile rose in my throat. My stomach churned and no matter how rigid I held my body, I started to shake when I remembered the thick taste of my fear and the loathing they leveled on me. "Their final humiliation was they each pretended to fuck me. Grinding their groins against my ass, pumping their hips into my face. Tellin' me I deserved to choke to death on a dick. Askin' if that was how I liked to get fucked. Calling' me a filthy butt fucker, a disgusting ass licker, a sinning sodomite, a cocksucking pervert…"

Cres rolled me over and wrapped himself around me. "Stop," he said hoarsely. "Take a break. Jesus, Breck, you're shaking like you're about to go into shock." He pulled the covers over us. "C'mere. For chrissake, let me warm you up."

I pressed my cheek against Cres's chest, letting the steady beat of his heart calm me.

That gave me the courage to skip to the end. "After these guys I'd once considered friends finished mentally brutalizing me, they kicked me a few times for good measure. My lip was split open. One of my eyes had already swollen shut. They left me tied up, helpless and bleeding in the dirt. I don't know how long I laid out there, but eventually I wiggled around enough to free my head from the blanket. I managed to stumble to the back door of the restaurant. I refused to let them call the cops. I'd walked to the diner from my hotel, so no way in hell was I goin' back there in case those fuckers had followed me. I called a cab to take me to my motor home I'd left at a campground outside of town. I guess I passed out after I crawled in bed.

"I woke up feverish. I went to one of those walk-in emergency clinics, got the infected wounds cleaned up, and they gave me antibiotics. After that…I must've slept for three damn days. But not long enough for the marks to scab over. I ended up with these scars."

Cres didn't say anything for the longest time.

But I wasn't panicked he'd pass judgment on me.

Finally he said, "I know gay-bashing happens." He pressed his lips to the top of my head. "I hate that it happened to you. *Hate* it."

"But?"

"But I have to ask why you even considered takin' this job. You're training guys whose main goal in life is to compete in the CRA—the organization that supports fuckers like the ones who destroyed your career and physically attacked you. After all you told me about driving under the radar and steering clear of the rodeo life that turned you into a guy you didn't recognize, why didn't you tell the Gradskys to suck it?"

"I like your dirty euphemisms, Cres."

"Answer the question."

I sat up. "Sutton asked me the same question this mornin'."

"What did you tell him?"

"It's not like I have another skill set besides rodeoin'."

Cres sat up too. "Bullshit. You have a college degree. There are a lot of other things you could do."

"Name one."

"Go to work for Stirling. You're a farmer with an Ag degree. You're perfect for her operation."

"I'd considered that. But she needs someone full time and permanent. I already told you I'm not a permanent guy. Itchy feet, transient nature, remember?"

That startled him. "Yeah, I remember."

"Spending three months in Colorado during the summer and bein' able to leave when the snow starts to fly appealed to me. Havin' a chance to mold a few of the guys in this younger generation appealed to me too. If they see me as a normal guy tryin' to make a livin', not the secretly gay former rodeo champion rocked by scandal...maybe I can make a difference and change their misperceptions."

"Christ, you're as altruistic as Mick."

Had he meant that as an insult?

"When do you start teaching?"

"Next week. I'm nervous as hell."

Cres scooted off the bed and started to get dressed. "I imagine you have set hours?"

"It's pretty fluid. I have specific things I'm talkin' about and then the other instructors and I are in group sessions with all the students. Berlin is emphasizing that we're a team."

"You don't agree with that philosophy?"

I watched him zip his jeans and fasten his belt. There was nothing sexier than a man wearing just a pair of jeans, his chest and feet bare. And Cres epitomized sexy with his ropy forearms, and long and lean build.

"Breck?"

My gaze traveled up his body until my eyes met his. "I've got it bad for you, rancher. You slipped those jeans on and all I can think about is tearing them off again."

He crawled across the mattress until we were face to face. "I've got it bad for you too, farmboy. So the point of all of my questions was to figure out when we're gonna see each other."

I said, "And?" because I knew there was something else on his mind.

"And if we're keeping this *9 ½ Weeks* just between us?"

"I'm not hedging, but a lot of this is a day-by-day, wait-and-see thing. My coworkers know I'm gay. If the students ask I'll be honest with them. But to me there's a difference between sayin' I'm involved with a guy and havin' a boyfriend who's part of my workin' life. Especially when I ain't exactly sure what all that workin' life entails." I reached up and ran my knuckles down his jaw. "I want to see you, to get to know you better, take full advantage of the time I'm here. So I don't have a problem with your truck bein' parked at my campsite. I don't care if the Gradskys know we're spending time together. If you wanna tell your brothers, I'm fine with that too. My natural reaction is to admit I want to keep you here in my bed and to shut out the world. That's the way I've always done things.

So this bein' out and proud thing…I'm more inclined to take baby steps than a giant leap."

Cres beamed at me. "Right answer."

I let out a relieved breath.

"Now get dressed. You promised to cook supper and I worked up an appetite fucking you stupid."

Chapter Six

Cres

As I entered the gates of the Grade A complex, I waved to Tammy and Trent, who were out for their pre-dinner walk.

I stopped to let Annie and her black lab, Shadow, cross the road.

Bill flagged me down and asked if my hardware store had a decent parts department since he was having a devil of a time getting what he needed from his local Mom and Pop place.

I slowed when I reached the recreation area.

Two groups of boys were shooting hoops on the basketball court.

Half a dozen girls played sand volleyball.

Most of the boys were more interested in watching the girls' parts bounce than they were in bouncing the ball.

I waved to Mitzi and Bob in the feed truck, who were making the rounds and feeding the stock.

Breck and I had been involved for four weeks. Since I was here almost every night after work, I'd become familiar with the facility and the staff.

So far Breck had an easier go of being the "gay" bulldogging instructor than he'd expected.

But if he did have problems, would he tell you?

That...I wasn't sure of.

Sexually, we meshed. It helped we were both horny as fuck all the time. The newness of being lovers hadn't worn off and the heat between us hadn't cooled a bit. In fact, now that we knew each other's preferences and kinks, we were even more eager to get naked and raunchy. Even with all of that…we were keeping it just sex between us.

Sure you are. That's why you know the comings and goings of ninety percent of the staff. That's why you keep his refrigerator stocked with groceries since he cooks supper for you almost every night. That's why your toiletries are in his bathroom. That's why you ironed his work shirts when he didn't have time. That's why you surprised him with a PlayStation since you hate gaming on his Xbox. That's why you've stopped running unless the two of you are running together. You're doing all of that stuff because it's keeping it "just sex" between you.

I shot a quick look at the envelope on the seat.

Undeniable proof, bud, that you've gone over for the man. If this was just a sexual relationship with an end date, you wouldn't need to get blood tests done so you can ditch the condoms.

Annoying that the voice of reason picked today to point that out. Even more annoying that I'd chosen this day to listen to it.

I'd been so adamant about not starting a relationship—even after Breck had pointed out "just sex" was a relationship. I'd naively believed I could keep feelings out of the equation. That physical release would be enough. Like I could get off and get gone.

Right.

I got off plenty. I just couldn't seem to yank up my boxer briefs after we finished fucking and get gone. I liked Breck, and spending time with him clothed held almost as much appeal as being body to body, skin to skin, mouth to mouth with him. We'd been able to build on, expand, and go beyond the physical attraction. The caring, open, and honest person Breck had become following his long journey to his self-acceptance was just the damn cherry on top. Yet, within those changes, he'd retained his sense of humor and his pride that he wasn't just a dumb cowboy. Seeing him transform from a selfish guy into a thoughtful man blew my mind. He pulled me out of the dark place I'd been in for too long, but he let me decide when I was ready to cross the next boundary. He remained by my side as I approached another hurdle—stopping the guilt because I was alive and Mick wasn't. That I deserved a second chance at happiness.

I wanted that happiness with him.

So he'd helped me come to terms with aspects of myself and my life that I could change….how did I help him see that by jumping back on the road when the semester ended, that he was hiding as much as I'd been? How did he know he wouldn't like a more settled life if he never tried it?

Not something I could solve today, but hopefully each day we spent together would make him want more days until he couldn't see a day without me in it. Because that's where I was.

I pulled up to the office building and parked. Sutton had sent a box of paperwork for me to deliver to Berlin since both London and Brennen were down with a stomach bug.

Berlin and Chuck bounded down the steps before I'd reached the end of the sidewalk.

"Here, lemme take that," Chuck said, plucking the box from my hands. "We appreciate you bringing this by."

"No problem. I'm usually in the neighborhood."

Chuck smiled. "And we're happy to have you here, Cres."

As soon as my hands were empty, Berlin hugged me. This family was the hugging-est bunch I'd ever met. "Have you seen my daughter and grandson?"

"Sutton is keeping them quarantined. This stomach flu is nasty stuff. It knocked him down for a week."

"I'm not surprised London and Brennen caught it."

"Us either. Luckily, Wyn, Mel, and Evan haven't been around them for a couple of weeks. It's hard on my folks, though. But we don't need them getting sick."

"Amen to that." Berlin's eyes scanned my face. "No one is worried about you catching it?"

I grinned. "My family claims I'm too ornery to catch it."

"Then London shouldn't have gotten it either."

"Ooh, I'm tellin' her you said that, Mama B."

She whapped me on the arm. "Come on. I know why you're really here. I want to see it too, so let's walk over to the arena."

Tonight the instructors were demonstrating their rodeo skills for their students. As much as I wanted to see my man in action, we were still stumbling our way through public appearances as a couple, especially when it came to his job. It'd been really sweet that the big, tough rodeo cowboy had acted shy when he'd asked me to come to the demo. As if I could refuse that.

It's not like you can refuse him anything.

Maybe I'll start with refusing to let him go when this session ended in six weeks.

Whatcha think about that, voice of reason?

My voice of reason got suspiciously quiet.

"So we received some great news today that you'll be interested to hear about."

Please tell me that Breck signed on for another teaching session.

"What's that?"

"Mel's sister Aly has agreed to teach an equestrian class next semester!"

I stepped around a cactus. "Mel will be thrilled. But is Grade A set up to handle that? I mean, is there specialized equipment you'll have to buy?"

"Believe it or not, Aly is donating most of it. And because this whole complex is brand new, it's completely ADA compliant."

My sister-in-law's sister Aly had been paraplegic since age sixteen. Being wheelchair bound hadn't prevented her equestrian pursuits. The woman was a total badass on a horse. After winning a bronze and a silver medal, last year she'd finally won gold in the Paralympics Games. Earlier this year Mel mentioned Aly had decided to retire from professional competition, but she wasn't sure what Aly would do next.

"We will have to change a couple of things," Berlin continued. "Starting with adding asphalt paths that connect all of the outer buildings to the arenas. It'd be too dangerous for wheelchairs to use the road."

"Aly has the contacts to bring in students?"

"Yes. But for that program, enrollment will be very limited. If it's successful we can always bump up the numbers."

I draped my arm over her shoulder. "Mama B, you are amazing. The more time I spend here, the more I'm impressed by the kind of place you've built. Not in terms of the best of everything—although that does apply—but it's an inclusive atmosphere when it could easily be exclusive. High-five for that."

Berlin stopped and faced me. "Thank you. It's been a labor of love."

"It shows."

We walked into the arena and I wasn't sure where I was supposed to go.

"Breck said you should sit at the rear since that's where you prefer to be."

I fought a blush. That jackass loved to tease and see if others picked up on his innuendo. "Thanks."

Berlin jogged down front and I scaled the bleachers until I reached the top row. I'd have a great view from here.

The kids I'd seen shooting hoops and playing volleyball started shuffling in. I watched DiDi, head chaperone, count heads and then do a roll call. When she spoke into her walkie-talkie, I suspected some dumb kid had tried to skip out.

I settled in to watch the show and snickered when Macon Gradsky's voice boomed through the sound system. It killed me that the buttoned-up attorney was a total ham when he filled in as an emcee, rodeo announcer, and DJ.

The school ran these demos like a rodeo, with the bucking horses first. The only difference was they'd do two run-throughs, allowing each instructor to demonstrate twice. I'd learned from Breck these past few weeks that rodeo competitors were making constant adjustments. Arena conditions, the quality level of the rough stock events impacted each round. So showing the students two rounds allowed them to see successes and failures—another unique aspect of this particular rodeo school.

Since Breck had stopped vying for the All-Around title after winning three world championships, he'd dropped saddle bronc from his competitive events. I was glad I didn't have to watch him tie himself to a mean-tempered bronc determined to toss him on his ass. Seeing him launch his big body off a galloping horse and onto an animal running away from him and then wrestling it to the ground provided enough white-knuckle moments for me.

I hadn't seen him compete in tie-down roping, but his championship status indicated he excelled at that too. Two nights ago the cheeky asshat had told me after he'd blown me that tie-down roping was the only real skill he could bring to ranch work.

So my head had been spinning, my balls were still tight, my cock was still throbbing when he'd dropped that gem on me. Or had it been a hint? Like he'd wanted me to be aware that he had the experience I needed in a ranch hand? Or was it wishful thinking that my lover was showing interest in becoming a long-term partner with a rancher?

I still hadn't sorted all that out yet.

Macon's announcement that Breck Christianson, three-time CRA All-Around World Champion, was on deck to demonstrate steer wrestling—aka bulldoggin' in the world of rodeo—pulled me out of the fantasy of Breck riding the range beside me for many years to come.

I squinted at the chute below me. On the left side I could see the top of Breck's hat and the ears of his horse. I didn't know who'd agreed to be his hazer—the guy riding on the right side during the run that kept Breck's horse in a straight line—but I knew he preferred to have Sutton doing it.

The gate opened, the steer got a head start, and then Breck chased after him.

My gut clenched when Breck leaned over the right side of his horse, with just his right foot in the stirrup and his left hand on the saddle horn. His left leg practically stuck straight up as he slid it across the back of the saddle.

Most people thought bulldoggers launched themselves forward, but they actually leaned back. So once they grabbed ahold of the steers' head, they could pull backward when both their feet hit the dirt. That balance to power ratio allowed them to twist their bodies and use their weight and strength to slam the steer on its side.

I'd listened to my brother discuss dismount strategies, complain about flexibility training and conditioning. I understood there was more to what steer wrestlers did than what rodeo spectators saw in the few seconds they spent in the arena.

When it all came together like clockwork? It was a sight to behold. Danger and precision that looked effortless.

That's how my man's first run went.

Breck had that steer down in 3.9 seconds.

Applause and whistles echoed throughout the arena. I had such a burst of pride for him to hear the entire school's acknowledgment of his skill—an affirmation he hadn't heard for far too long.

I saw him glance at the judge to see if there were flags for breaking the barrier or an illegal takedown. When he saw nothing but the impressive time on the scoreboard, his cocky grin made my dick hard.

And I paid particular attention to how he walked across the dirt. Not only because his rear view was damn fine with that tight cowboy ass and his broad shoulders, but I wanted to see if he favored his right leg. He'd mentioned having a sore knee last night. When I saw him hitch his shoulders and twist to the side, I figured he'd probably prefer a backrub to a blowjob tonight.

My voice of reason snorted disbelief.

After the bulldogging event was tie-down roping, and I noticed Breck served as hazer for the tie-down roper. Team roping followed, then barrel racing, and finally bull riding.

There was a fifteen-minute intermission before the next round started. I didn't move, although I exchanged a few friendly waves with other instructor's significant others as we killed time in the stands.

Breck's second run resulted in just a tenth of a second faster than his first time. If this was a real competition, his combined score was good enough to land him in the payout slots.

After the demo ended, a quick thank-you to teachers served as the closing of the event. The arena emptied quickly but I didn't rush out. Breck would track me down when he finished with his official duties. The school had horse handlers, so he didn't have to deal with that, but he never trusted anyone to take care of his tack—a habit I respected.

Twenty minutes later I heard the *clang clang* of his boot heels on the metal steps as he climbed the risers. The happy grin, the light shining in his eyes when he looked at me...just did me in.

Yep. You are so dick-whipped over this bulldogger.

I stood when he reached me. He didn't look over his shoulder to see if anyone was watching before he hooked his hand around the back of my neck and brought my mouth to his for a kiss.

"Hey."

Another thing that made me so crazy about him? He kissed me hello. Every single time. Usually before he uttered "hey"—the standard cowboy greeting.

"Hey, yourself. Nice runs. You looked good. Smooth. Like you're still competing a few times a week."

He shrugged, but I knew he was pleased I'd mentioned it. "Thanks. You hungry?"

"Starved."

"Good. I had a little extra time today so I went into town and picked up that ice cream you like so much."

"You did?"

"Yep. Course, you're gonna have to share."

A mental image flashed of Breck licking the sweet white stuff off my stomach and cock.

"I also saw the new Lee Child paperback, so I snagged that for you too."

Yeah. Not just about sex for me anymore—if it ever was. "Aw. Thanks. Is that a hint you need a break tonight and you're actually gonna let me read?"

Breck growled and gave me a hard kiss. "Fuck, no. We're gonna eat. Then fuck. Then I'm gonna school you on Madden, boy."

"You wish. I have a surprise for you too."

"What?"

"Not telling. That's why it's a surprise."

He shrugged. "I know what it is anyway. Blood test results."

Of course he'd gotten his too. "Mine were all clear. I brought them with me."

"Mine's all clear too."

We grinned at each other.

Then he said, "Think it'd be obvious we're impatient to fuck if we run through the crowd and back to the campsite?"

"Maybe just a tad. Besides, I'll meet you. I left my truck in the office parking lot."

"I'll walk with you."

I didn't point out that would put us in direct view of the cafeteria and the dorms and everyone would know we were headed back to his place.

But Mr. Popular had to stop and chat with everyone. As much as I wanted time alone with him, it thrilled me to see the return of charismatic Breck, the confident cowboy, the guy in the thick of things. The joy on his face, like he truly felt their acceptance…was worth the wait.

Chapter Seven

Breck

"I suck as a teacher."

Jerry, my colleague, the saddle bronc instructor, grunted and crushed his empty Coors can beneath his boot. "What makes you think that? Did one of your students say something to you?"

"No. It just seems none of them are makin' any progress."

"Progress." Jerry snorted. "These kids are here to learn the basics. Think back to when you were seventeen. Did you give a hoot about *makin' progress*? Or were you more focused on if the pretty girls were watching you acting like a rodeo cowboy stud?"

A beat of silence passed and the campfire popped, sending a flame of orange sparks into the air.

"Shoot. Sorry. Sometimes I forget that you're…" He gestured distractedly. "You know."

I grinned. "You have no idea how happy I am to hear you say that you forgot I'm…*you know…*"

"Smarty."

"Anyway, yeah, I had an ego and liked people watching me become a rodeo stud and All-Around Cowboy contender. But I also had discipline and drive to get better in all three of my events. And I can't get these boys to focus on just one event when they're in class."

"Discipline and drive is why you've won more championships than the whole lot of these students—combined—ever will." He paused. "There's only one student here with the potential to win big."

We both said, "Etta Geyer," at the same time.

"See? You know talent when you see it, Breck. You can't feel guilty because none of your kids have talent."

"Lucky for Sharla, she knows she's got a gem in Etta." Sharla, the barrel racing instructor, had twenty years on me and Jerry age wise. She'd retired from competition before I'd started competing. I'd never met anyone who knew every nuance of the sport like she did.

"Etta may have to give it up because of her family situation." Jerry cracked open another Coors. "I ain't a gossiping old fart, but this is her last year to prove herself on her high school team and snag the eye of one of them college rodeo team recruiters."

"Where's she from?"

"Nebraska."

"So she lives too far to use Gradskys' stock to make a splash."

"Yep. Damn shame. But I think the school officials would call it an unfair advantage." He sent me a sideways glance. "Etta's been clocked below eleven on Whistler's Dream."

I shook my head. "That's unheard of."

"That's why I hope that little gal gets to make a name for herself."

We watched the fire for a while. I kicked the closest charred log deeper into the embers.

Jerry swallowed a mouthful of beer. "The last three weeks of this session are gonna drag out forever."

God, I hoped so. I couldn't believe how fast time had flown by and I'd been in Colorado for two months. Cres and I had been together for seven of those eight weeks. When I realized I only had three more weeks with him, tightness banded across my chest and I felt as if I was slowly suffocating.

"If you think you're a sucky teacher, does that mean you won't be back next session?"

I wasn't sure how to answer.

Then Jerry's cell phone rang. He said, "Sorry, I gotta take this," and swung his legs over the other side of the log, disappearing into the darkness.

Staring into the flames, I brooded about my uncertain future. I didn't trust my ambivalence toward teaching because I was a master at self-sabotage. Maybe I considered this teaching experiment a failure so I had an excuse not to sign on for the next session. Then I could stick with the

"I'm a ramblin' man" warning I'd given Cres and return to the blacktop.

But I didn't want to go back on the road. Facing miles of empty highway day after day...I knew firsthand it was as lonely as it sounded.

Loneliness hadn't been an issue since I'd rolled into the Grade A complex. I spent my days surrounded by students and staff and my nights wrapped up in Cres.

Sexy, funny, sweet Cres.

I'd been such a fool to think I could work him out of my system. The more time we spent together the more I wanted. Yet Cres hadn't mentioned extending our time.

Maybe because you've done a bang-up job convincing him of your "itchy feet."

Only because he'd been so insistent about never getting into another serious relationship, and I didn't want to be the pathetic hanger-on, trying to convince him that I was worth the risk to his heart, because I wasn't sure I was.

There was some confidence. I'd gotten my mo-jo back in the arena, but I didn't have the same certainty with Cres unless I was fucking him.

Why did this have to be so fucked up? Why couldn't I just tell him my feelings had changed and I needed more than "just sex?"

Because I was worried that his feelings hadn't changed. He'd made some strides in letting go of his guilt for moving on from Mick, but I knew he was still hung up on the guy. In all the weeks we'd been together, Cres hadn't asked me to sleep over at his house. Which made no sense...unless he considered the bedroom he'd shared with Mick a sacred place he never wanted to share with another man. By denying me access to his personal space, he believed he was keeping to his original declaration he didn't want anything but a physical relationship.

As much as it bugged me that I hadn't gotten an invite into his bed, I had too much fucking pride to ask for one.

Boot steps stomping across the underbrush had me shaking off the melancholy. I expected to see Jerry reappear, but Macon stepped out of the dark woods.

"Breck! What are you doin' out here?"

"Enjoying the campfire, the stars, and the clean Colorado air." *While I'm wallowing in uncertainty of where "what is" intersects with "what could be."*

Jesus. Where had that hippie-dippy philosophy come from? I sounded like I'd been sampling some of their product.

Macon eyed Jerry's empty beer can. "Are you enjoying an icy cold beer? Because I'd take one if you were offering."

"Sorry. Fresh out."

"I forget you're a teetotaler now."

I shrugged. "I don't miss it, to be honest. I really don't miss the bad decisions I made when I was liquored up." I'd been hesitant to mention my non-drinker status to Cres, but he'd been fully supportive. He didn't drink around me—his choice, not something I'd asked of him. He'd told me he'd rather have the taste of me in his mouth than beer anyway.

"I hear ya. So where's Cres?"

"At his home, I reckon. Why?"

He lowered onto the log. "No reason. You two are usually joined at the hip."

"He's hit the busy season at the ranch now, so he'll be around less."

"Sucks for you," Macon said. "So what's this bullshit I've heard from Mom that you're not re-upping to teach next session?"

"I'm not...*not* re-upping. I haven't decided yet."

"No need to get defensive. I get that dealing with teens isn't for everyone. I thought you'd give it more than one session. Especially now that you've found someone worth sticking around for."

"Me'n Cres haven't discussed makin' this relationship permanent, so we'll see."

"Yeah, right." Macon smirked. "After seeing you two together, you're feeling the burning need to go back on the road?"

I didn't need him grilling me on things that were already pissing me off. "What are you doin' here, counselor?"

"Babysitting, apparently."

"Lemme guess. Stirling and Liam got into it again."

He touched his nose.

"What is the deal with them?"

"They were both used to bein' the alpha dog in their previous positions and neither is willing to be the beta even for one damn day." He pinned me with a look. "Organic farming was my little sister's bright idea, not mine. If I had my way, we'd use that acreage for pot. But it's too late in the season to build grow houses. If she intends to plant anything next season, she has to prep that soil now before it snows so it's ready to go in the spring."

"What needs done before it's ready to go?"

"Plowing, tilling, taking soil samples, figuring out what needs to be added to adjust the PH levels for each heirloom variety. Hiring a certifying agent. But instead of getting a jump on that, she thought it'd be funny to put powdered purple Kool-Aid in Liam's favorite lab gloves."

I winced. "Shit."

"Yeah. His hands are stained the most hideous shade of purple. She bought him new gloves only after I chewed her ass, but she refused to apologize. She said he needs to grow a sense of humor. Then she added that next time she'll dump blue powder in his cup." He sighed. "Now I have to worry how Liam will retaliate, because there's no way he'll let this slide."

Kool-Aid reminded me of the summers I'd spent toiling on the farm in South Dakota. I'd never minded the work—it was working with family that drove me away. I'd known from age ten that I wanted to rodeo and farm, so I'd practiced my rodeo skills during the day and pored over Ag magazines at night. I'd taken great satisfaction in the purple ribbons I'd won in 4H and for FFA at the state fair for the produce I'd grown in my section.

"What were you thinking about just now?" Macon asked.

"Sorry." I shot him a sheepish look. "Didn't mean to tune you out. I was just thinkin' about farming and college. Lost opportunities."

"Or ones that were taken from you?"

"I've had enough distance to admit that goin' back home and helping run the family farm hadn't ever been in the cards for me."

Macon leaned forward, resting his forearms on his knees. "So if you really hate teaching, would you consider coming to work for us on the organic farming side of Grade A?"

"You askin' me because you wanna pass off the babysitting duties?"

He laughed. "I'm pleading the fifth on that one. But I am serious because if you would've said no to the rodeo school, I planned to ask if you'd be interested in the Ag side."

Maybe I did have options besides hitting the happy trail to nowhere. "Why?"

"I've known you since college. I trust you and you've got the background to be a real asset. And I don't think you'll find anyplace else that suits you better on a personal level either. You have acceptance and respect here, Breck. That's something you were looking for the past couple of years."

He'd poked every one of my "Yes! Where do I sign?" buttons. That was the perfect example of Macon being the Gradskys' secret weapon in negotiations; he wouldn't walk away unless he got what he wanted.

Maybe you should adopt that philosophy.

"I'll think about it."

A log popped with enough force it sounded like a gunshot and I jumped.

"Is this a private party?"

I jumped again and my head snapped up.

Cres stood on the other side of the campfire, his hands jammed in the front pockets of his jeans.

Macon chuckled and stood. "It is now."

"Hey, Macon. How's it goin'?" Cres asked.

"I can't complain. How've you been?"

"Busy and cranky."

Macon pointed at me. "Maybe you can pull each other out of your bad moods." He hopped over the log and vanished into the forest.

I refocused on Cres. Firelight created a glow as if he were a mythical woodland creature.

"You're lookin' at me like I'm a ghost, Breck."

"Since I hadn't expected to see you tonight, I worried you were just an apparition I'd conjured up."

"Nope. I'm flesh and blood and bone."

I cocked my head. "Did you say you had a boner?"

He laughed. "Not yet."

"The night is still young." Except it wasn't. It was after eleven and past the time early rising ranchers were usually in bed. "So you were in the neighborhood?"

Cres plopped down on the log across from me. "Nah. I was restless. So I took a drive."

"And ended up here." Why? Because he wanted to watch the next episode of *Archer* on Netflix with me? For a fast goodnight fuck to take off the restless edge?

If he was here to get fucked, I'd oblige him. Happily. At least twice if he did a little sweet talkin'. Or better yet, dirty talkin'.

Then he shocked the hell out of me by saying, "I took a drive here because I missed you, dumbass."

The tightness in my chest loosened. I crooked my finger at him. "Prove it."

He sauntered over, intending to sit next to me.

"Huh-uh. Down there"—I pointed to the ground—"so I can put my hands on you."

"Bossy bulldogger wants me worshipping at his feet," he said with a sly grin. "Not a surprise." He situated himself between my legs, propping his forearms on my thighs.

"Forget something?"

Cres tilted his head back. "What?"

"This." I lowered my lips to his and we kissed for a good long time. We needed that connection since Cres's working hours had kept us apart of late.

"This is romantic," he said softly.

"Only now that you're here." I leaned closer. "I wanna fuck you by a fire sometime. I'll bet your ass looks hot with a red glow to it."

Cres cranked his head around and narrowed his eyes at me. "Was that a hint that you want to spank me? Get my ass glowing red from these big hands of yours?"

"No. I never wanna hit you. Even when it's supposed to be fun or hot and sexy or whatever." The idea of touching him with anything except reverence—even the roughness that exploded between us wasn't borne out of violence but passion—turned my stomach.

"Hey. I'd never ask that of you, okay?"

Sensing my tension, he nuzzled the inside of my thigh until I relaxed and said, "Okay."

"I'd like to see you nekkid by firelight too, farmboy."

"Maybe someday soon we'll both get our wish." I laced our fingers together and rested our joined hands on my knees. I dropped my chin onto the top of his head. "So tell me about your day, rancher."

As Cres filled me in with the details about his long-assed day, while he was warm and pliant in my arms, I had a sense of rightness I hadn't felt...maybe ever.

And I knew I'd do whatever it took to keep it.

Chapter Eight

Cres

Buzzing on the nightstand at four a.m. woke me and it wasn't the alarm on my phone. I immediately reached for my cell and blinked at the caller ID.

Wyn.

"Bro, did you butt dial me again when you got up with Evan?" I said groggily.

"No. Melissa's water broke."

The panic in my brother's voice had me sitting up. "She's not due for another two months."

"I know. I'm dropping Evan off with Sutton and London and takin' her to the hospital."

"What can I do?"

"I don't know when I'll be back so you'll probably be doin' everything by yourself the next couple of days at least."

"Wyn, I'll be fine. Take care of your wife and baby."

He blew out a breath. "I'm not calling Mom and Dad—no reason to wake them up when there's nothin' they can do. I'll give them an update when I know more."

"Sounds good. Keep in touch as best as you can. Give Mel my love."

"I will. Thanks." He hung up.

I eased back down into the pillows, but I was wide awake and worried so it'd be pointless to try to go back to sleep. I got up, dressed, and shuffled to the kitchen to make coffee. Guess I'd get chores done early today.

If you're doing them by yourself? Wrong.

In the past four years since our dad had retired and turned the ranch over to us, Wyn and I had doubled our herd. We'd leased grazing land instead of buying it outright to see how difficult a larger herd was to manage. Some times of the year one person could handle it all. But this time of year, Wyn and I both could stay busy from sunup to sundown. After Mick died, I'd willingly taken on more responsibilities because working until exhaustion had been easier than being alone in an empty house.

Before I'd met Mick it hadn't bothered me to live alone.

That's because you hadn't known what you were missing.

Over the past few weeks that Breck and I had been together, I'd realized he'd exaggerated his contentment about being a lone wolf. We were together nearly every night. If we weren't physically in the same space, we were on the phone. Or texting.

The pink and orange glow of sunrise spread across the horizon as I started down the porch steps. Banjo greeted me, his tail wagging crazily. I scratched behind his ears. "Let's get you fed so we can start the day."

He yipped in agreement.

I finished my coffee as Banjo chowed down. It'd be faster to check the herd on horseback than going over to Wyn's and getting out a 4-wheeler. Then I could return for the truck before I started baling the grass we'd cut last week. I hoped the baler cooperated. Damn thing was old and touchy as hell. Only Wyn seemed to have the magic touch with it. We were babying it, trying to eke one last season out of it before we upgraded.

Banjo scrambled down the steps and rolled in the dirt. Then he shook himself and barked at me.

"Okay, okay, let's get Petey saddled and we'll be on our way to check cattle."

Had I always talked to my dog this much?

Yes. Mick complained you talked to the dog more than you talked to most people.

For the first time in a long time, thinking about Mick didn't cause me pain.

Hours later, I returned to the house and checked my cell phone for news from Wyn. Sure enough, he'd left me a voice mail. As had Sutton. And my dad.

Shit.

I listened to Wyn's message first.

"Hey. I'll get to the point since I ain't got a lot of time. The docs performed an emergency C-section. They put Melissa out for it and she's still in recovery with some minor complications. Since the baby was eight weeks early and he only weighed two pounds, and he'd gone into distress prior to birth, and there's no neonatal care unit here, they immediately flew him to Denver Children's via Life Flight. Melissa can't travel after the surgery for several days, depending on when they get her blood sugar levels managed and her blood pressure stabilized. Which means I'm on my way to Denver right now to be with the baby. I had to leave Melissa here. Christ, I didn't even get to see her, Cres. And neither of us has even seen our son."

My guts twisted at hearing the anguish in his voice.

"Between Sutton and London and Mom and Dad, Evan will be looked after. I hate for Melissa to be alone in the hospital, but she needs to take advantage of this time and freakin' rest. So I'm sorry, bro, but you'll be a one-man band while I'm dealing with all the family medical stuff."

Like that was something he needed to worry about with his premature baby in one hospital and his wife in another.

"Text me when you get a chance and I'll check in later when I know more."

I saved the message and played the one from Sutton.

"Hey, Cres, I know Wyn called and filled you in on what's goin' on. I don't have anything new to report except to say holler if you need help. I'm sure you'll be hearing from Dad and he'll try and convince you he's up to the task of mowing, but he's not and we all know it."

My dad had been a rancher all his life until a heart attack had forced him into early retirement. We'd had to adjust our lives then, and it looked to be the same thing now.

"Mom will be helping London out with the boys as well as spending time with Melissa in the hospital. Once Melissa is able to go to Denver, Dad will drive her. If we keep Dad busy then he won't insist on helping you with ranch work. Sucks, but it'd be best for everyone if you're on your own."

No shit.

"Anyway, Wyn forgot to tell you your nephew's name is Truman. It's hard for him to stop calling Tru 'the baby' since they weren't ready for him and it'll be touch and go as far…his odds. But the sooner we all call Truman by his name, the more it'll show the world that we believe he's a fighter and he *is* gonna make it. He has to make it. Has to."

Sutton's voice broke on the last couple of words.

"Text me when you get back from checking cattle."

I saved Sutton's message and played my dad's next.

"Cres. I know what your brothers are doin' with havin' me be a glorified damn gopher and chauffeur—tryin' to keep me from helping you on the ranch. But if you have problems with the baler, call me. If you need a gate opener, call me. I'm not a damn invalid."

That made me smile.

After I slapped together a couple of sandwiches, I hitched the baler to my truck and headed out.

Luck was on my side and the baler didn't break down. I finished the last bale just before sunset.

On the way home I managed to talk to both of my brothers and my parents. No change in Truman's condition was considered good news because they'd gotten him stabilized. And Mel had been moved into a regular room—more good news.

I hesitated to call Breck. This was the last week of class and he'd warned me his schedule would be tight. I missed him.

Our agreement of no relationship and just indulging in a nine-week fuckfest…had lasted maybe one night. The last couple times we'd hung out, we hadn't fucked. We binge watched two seasons of Breck's new obsession *American Ninja Warrior*.

He'd tried to teach me how to roll a poker chip through my fingers. When he questioned my dexterity after the hundredth unsuccessful attempt, I proved my dexterity was above average with an outstanding hand job.

After that he hadn't uttered a single crack about my fumbling fingers.

He'd even set up a moonlit horseback ride for us. Breck had a romantic streak, which I loved, but he also balanced that with his dirty, adventurous side. He'd fucked me with such possession and intensity I'd had a hard time getting back on the horse.

I loved every second of it.

Shaking off that train of thought, I left the baler hooked up to my truck and trudged into my house. Exhaustion set in as soon as I took my boots off. I conked out on the couch in front of the TV.

The next morning I woke up starving since I'd skipped supper. Banjo whined at the door. I'd forgotten to feed him too. "I'm coming, dog."

Day two was nearly identical to day one.

The next three days were a blur of work and family phone calls.

The fifth day Breck pulled up at dawn just as I exited the house.

My belly fluttered and I felt a ridiculous sense of happiness that he was here.

Banjo yipped and jumped all over Breck as soon as he got out of his Jeep.

Smart dog. I wished I could get away with being all over Breck too.

My eyes drank him in because my man looked like a million bucks in faded jeans, a long-sleeved plaid shirt, and a cream-colored summer-weight cowboy hat. His handsome face was smooth and his smile genuine as he petted my dog.

"You're a good boy, aren't you, Banjo?" He straightened and propped his hands on his hips. "The dog gave me a more enthusiastic welcome than you have. Oh, and he's texted me just as many times as you have too, Cres."

"Ha, ha. I've been busy, you know, running the ranch by myself and all."

When he started toward me, my pulse skyrocketed.

"Berlin told me some of what's goin' on." He stopped in front of me. "How are Mel and the baby?"

If I concentrated on answering, maybe I wouldn't be enticed by the scent of his cologne. "They're releasing Mel this morning, if her numbers hold up. Then my folks will drive her and Evan to Denver. Wyn's been there with Truman. Mel hasn't even seen him yet."

"Is the baby okay?"

"They're doin' everything they can to help him survive. He'll have a long stay in the hospital. So Wyn and Mel and Evan will be living in Denver until Tru is healthy and ready to come home." I sighed. "It's rough on everyone."

"I imagine. But it sounds as if it'll be really rough on you." That beautiful blue gaze encompassed my face. "You look like hell, Cres."

"Thanks, Captain Obvious."

"Here's something else that oughta be obvious—I'm pissed off at you. But before we get into that…" Breck curled his hand around the back of my neck. "I need this." He slanted his mouth over mine and kissed me. First with the passion that made breathing difficult, then with the sweet longing that had me swaying against him.

He didn't touch me except for maintaining the iron grip on my neck. But he held me one hundred percent in his thrall with just his kiss.

When he finally had his fill of the lip-lock, he buried his face in the crook of my neck. "Why didn't you call me? I've been worried about you and your family."

"Besides the fact you warned me not to bug you during this last week of the session?" *Besides the fact I worried you'd already heard the siren's call and had returned to your life on the road? And the thought of driving to the campground and finding you gone, like you'd done to me in Denver—made me physically ill?*

He lifted his head and blinked at me. "I don't remember sayin' that."

"You did."

"When?"

"The night we sat by the campfire with Stirling and Macon."

"I was in a sugar coma from those damn s'mores she insisted we eat and I wasn't thinking clearly."

"Or...they weren't s'mores at all, and those sneaky Gradskys were secretly product testing us."

"You were especially horny after that, so it's a possibility." Breck rubbed his mouth down my throat. "Fuck. I just want to take a bite outta you."

I groaned. "I'd let you bite me wherever you want, but once you start, I won't have the willpower to stop you."

"We'll pick this up later." He stepped back. "What are we doin' first today?"

I raised my chin to look at him. "We?"

"I'm here to help you."

"I don't need—"

"Bullshit. You do need me—would it kill you to admit it?"

Had he intended for that to have a double meaning?

You're exhausted, Cres. Let it go.

He cocked his head. "Okay, we'll talk about why you dodged that question also. Get it through that thick cowboy head of yours that I ain't goin' anywhere, so let's get this done. Cattle check first, right?"

I nodded.

"You still haying after that?"

"Yeah."

"I don't know that I'll be much help with the haying, but I can help with the cattle. Then later on we can get to the other reason I showed up at the crack of dawn."

"Which is what?"

"I missed you, dumbass."

I smiled. "Let's see if you can keep up, farmboy."

Breck flashed me that megawatt grin. "Bring it, rancher."

"You have your own tack?"

"Always. And don't even think about giving me a shitty old horse."

I raised an eyebrow. "Snobby about your horseflesh?"

"I'm used to the best."

"Unfortunately for you, the best is my horse Petey. You can't have him so you'll have to make do with second best."

"Better to make do than to be second best," he muttered.

I squinted at him. "What'd you say?"

"Nothin'. Let's round 'em up."

"We're not 'rounding them up,' bulldogger."

He smirked at me. "So it'd be against the rancher's handbook of clichés to say 'get along little doggie' to Banjo?"

"You are punchy."

"That's because I'm spending the day as a *cow puncher*."

"Jesus." I groaned. "I missed you."

Within the first half an hour of working with Breck, I knew two things. One, my cock would spend the next five hours in agony because watching him ride made me hard as a fucking fence post. And two, his abilities on a horse weren't just for show. He was a good ranch hand. I appreciated the fact he didn't yammer on and that he followed my directions.

Over the course of the morning, the sky had transformed from watery blue, to dismal gray to almost black. The air had cooled considerably and hung heavy with humidity.

"Let's try and beat the storm," I said just as the first fat raindrops fell.

"Too late," he said as the skies opened up.

Once we'd reached the barn, we took off the saddles and draped the tack over the sides of the pens. We brushed the horses down and turned them loose in the pasture.

I removed my wet hat and hung it on a peg. When I turned around, Breck was right there.

"Shame about the rain keeping you from haying this afternoon." The smolder in his eyes burned off any residual chill. "Yeah, I'm really broken up about it." I angled my head and licked a bead of water in the hollow of his throat. Then I attacked the buttons on his shirt. "You'd better get these wet clothes off." I pushed him against the support beam and sucked on his neck, grinding my groin into his.

He was already as hard as I was.

I peeled off his wet shirt. The nearly see-through undershirt clung to every ripple of muscle on his chest. I lowered my mouth to the dark nipple, the tip already hard enough to bite, and I started to suck through the fabric.

He hissed out a breath.

But when I began to work his belt, he stayed my hand.

I moved to the other nipple and knocked his hand away, reaching down to palm his cock.

Again, he pushed my hand aside.

I lifted my head and looked at him. "You got a problem with me touching you?"

Breck locked his frustrated gaze to mine. "No. Unless this is another attempt to keep us from finishing this inside. In the house you shared with Mick. In the bed you shared with him."

"Whoa." I stepped back. Way back. His accusation quickly snapped me out of my horny state. "What are you talkin' about?"

"Why haven't we ever fucked in your house? Goddammit, Cres, we've been together two and a half goddamned months and I've never made it past your front porch."

That startled me. "What? That's...not true." Or was it?

"Come on. You can't possibly be surprised by that," he snapped.

"Well, I am. I didn't realize we were supposed to be keeping track of our overnights on a calendar," I shot back.

"Maybe if we had, you'd see that yours is completely blank. You always come to my place, which is great because bein' with you is the high point of my day. Since you have to get up at the ass crack of dawn to do chores, wouldn't it make sense for you to ask me to spend the night here sometimes? But you've never asked me. Not one time."

I stared at him, absolutely poleaxed.

"I'd even gone so far as to justify your lack of an invite into your house and your bed as you avoiding a confrontation with Wyn. Bein's you ranch together, I imagine he's here early in the morning. If he saw my Jeep, then you'd have to confess you're fucking a guy he can't stand."

"How do you know that Wyn can't stand you?"

"Sutton told me." He snorted. "But it's never had a damn thing to do with Wyn. It has everything to do with Mick."

Goddammit. He could be so self-righteous…even when he was dead wrong. I got in his face. "I don't need this shit from you today."

"Tough. You're getting it. I'm tired of avoiding the ghost in the room. Or maybe I should say the damn ghost still living in your house."

He did *not* just say that.

"You're an asshole. And a fucking clueless one at that. Go home, Breck." Fuming, I spun on my heel and walked out.

From that first night, being with him had made me so happy that was all I focused on—getting to him as soon as my workday ended, seeing that special dirty smile as he leaned in the doorway of his motor home waiting for me. I hadn't cared where we were together, just that we *were* together.

I stepped outside. The gloomy angry sky fit my mood. The rain had gone from a steady drizzle to a torrential downpour.

I'd barely made it fifteen feet when a hand landed on my shoulder.

"Cres. Wait."

I turned to face him. "What?"

Even soaked to the skin, standing in the rain, Breck didn't look like a drowned rat; he looked like a male model at a photo shoot for a vacation in the tropics. Water streamed down the angles and planes of his face. Tiny droplets sparkled on the ends of his long eyelashes. His hair, without his cowboy hat to smash it down, had become a riot of black curls.

Yeah, he's gorgeous, but he's about to tear into you without just cause, so focus.

"Don't shut me down when I finally have the balls to admit that I'm jealous of him. He gets a place of honor in your house and I get the barn."

"Breck. What the hell are you even talkin' about?"

"I'm talkin' about you messing around with me in the barn because you don't want to bring me into your house—the sacred space you shared with him."

"Sacred space? That doesn't have fuck-all to do with anything. I wanted to mess around in the barn with you because nothin' like that ever happened with him."

I shouldn't have relished his expression of shock, but I did.

"I'm sick to death of keeping all this inside and worrying I'm tarnishing his memory by admitting the truth."

"What truth?"

"What you and I have? Passion, need, lust…I never had with him. Mick wasn't spontaneous or adventurous. It drove me crazy that he kept his military attitude even when it came to sex. We fucked on the bed in the bedroom—because that's where you were supposed to fuck. We might've had sex in the shower once, but he never would've blown me in the barn or the kitchen or the truck. He wouldn't have let me suck him off on the first fuckin' date, outside with a thousand people partying in a tent behind us. He had some rigid ideas about roles and refused to consider other options."

"Like what?"

"Like he bottomed. Period."

His eyes went wide with shock. "Mick never fucked you?"

I shook my head. "He said 'Not my thing' and that was that. We fought about it, but I knew he wouldn't change his mind."

"So you just accepted it?"

I looked away.

"Answer me."

"I accepted it then. I wouldn't now."

"Fuckin' *look* at me when you're talkin' to me."

My defiant gaze met his. "What do you want me to say?"

"The truth."

"The truth that I settled for Mick? Because it was easy and comfortable? Maybe I did. But it didn't feel like that at the time because I loved him." I ignored the pained look on Breck's face and soldiered on. "And bein' with you is different in every way I needed it to be. Nothing…no one…has ever come close to giving me what you do. No boundaries, no limits, and no goddamned way is it fair that I have to give it up."

"You are confusing the fuck outta me."

"What don't you understand? I don't want you to go. You know why you didn't hear from me this week? Besides the fact I was too damn tired to even take my boots off when I stumbled into my house at night? Because I was afraid you'd already moved on."

"Moved on," he repeated. "To another guy? Fuck you if you think I'd do that when—"

"Literally moved on, in your motor home, tooling down the road like you repeatedly warned me you planned to do as soon as your teaching job ended."

"I would never do that to you!" he yelled over the thunder.

"Bullshit. You did it to me in Denver. No note, no nothin'. You just hitched up your horse trailer and you were gone, Breck."

"I am not that guy anymore. And I'm still here."

"For how long?" I demanded. "Because I want this to be long-term with you—"

"Since when?" he demanded back. "You've never indicated anything has changed from the first time you told me about Mick. You've maintained that you never want another relationship."

"I didn't think I did, but fuck, *you're* the one who told me that us fucking made it a fucking relationship! So we've been in one from the start. And I don't want to give it up. *Ever.* Do you hear me? I want it all from you, Breck, not just sex. I'll buy medicated powder for your itchy feet if that's what it'll take to keep you here with me—"

His mouth crashed down on mine.

He devoured me.

Breck kissed me so often I thought I'd known every type of kiss in his arsenal.

But nothing that had been between us before had prepared me for this: his brutal, beautiful possession and his onslaught of emotion that transcended words.

I clung to him as if my life depended on it, because in a way it did.

When we came up for air, Breck curled his hands around my face. "Right here in the wind and the rain, in the mud, on my knees and on yours, I'm gonna give you what you want, Cres, and then I'm gonna take what I need."

"Breck, wait—"

But he didn't hear me—or didn't give a damn—because he was already on his knees, working my jeans open, yanking the wet denim down to my ankles.

Then his mouth hovered above my cock for the briefest moment.

I loved watching him blow me, seeing that beautiful face lost in bliss as my dick tunneled in and out of his hungry, sucking mouth.

He swallowed my cock in one greedy, suctioning pull, groaning like a starving man, and then it was on.

No teasing.

No finesse.

Just speed.

Lots and lots of speed.

I fisted his black silk curls and held on.

More thunder rumbled. Rain continued to beat at us. The wind rose and fell.

I came as quickly and with as much force as the storm.

Immediately Breck brought me to the ground in a show of dominance.

We rolled. Him on top, then me. Our bodies were bucking and grinding together as we fought each other.

Fighting for deeper kisses.

Fighting for a better position to taste and touch and bite.

I pulled his hair when he sucked on my neck.

His fingernails gouged my back when I gifted him with the same openmouthed suck mark.

Rain pounded down.

Thunder pounded above us.

Breck flipped me onto my knees and elbows, lifting my ass into the air, using a combination of spit and water as lube and then he was pounding into me.

I'd never been fucked with the elements leaving as much of a mark on me as my lover.

The air crackled—not with lightning but with the energy flowing between us.

He roared when he came.

I let him have his beastly moment.

Because I was going to get mine.

And I did.

I pushed him back, spun him around and pinned him down, driving my cock into his ass with the same driving force as the rain.

My body should've been cold after spending this much time in the rain, but I radiated heat.

And power.

God, I fucking loved this explosion of need between us that had us fucking in the mud.

After having *this*…I couldn't ever go back to not having it.

Breck bore down as I plowed into him.

One, two, three strokes and I erupted.

Water dripped into my mouth when I tipped my head back and howled to the sky.

As I caught my breath I half-expected—half-hoped?—Breck would be ready to go at me again.

But he grunted and bumped his ass into my thighs as a hint to climb off.

I pulled out and flopped on my back, closing my eyes.

Gravel crunched beside me and then it was quiet.

Breck spoke first. "You okay?"

"Fuck, no." I paused. "Are you?"

"Fuck, no."

I smiled and figured he was smiling too.

"Ask me again," I said a few moments later.

"Are you okay?"

"Fuck, yeah."

He snickered.

I said, "Are you okay?"

"Fuck, yeah."

I'd like to say we were smart enough to come out of the rain after that, but we weren't.

We didn't move.

Maybe because we couldn't move.

"You howled," he said almost conversationally.

"Your beast roars, mine howls. No fucking judgment, dude."

"Christ, I think I just fell in love with you."

"Ditto." I groaned. "I've never said ditto in my life."

Breck said, "Ditto."

That word struck me as wrong and funny. And I started laughing—the hold your gut, slap your knee, wipe your eyes kind of laughter.

"What's so funny?"

That almost set me off again. "Besides the fact we're both laying in a puddle on the driveway with our jeans around our knees, after we fucked each other so thoroughly during a thunderstorm that we can't even fucking crawl into the house?"

Next thing I knew Breck started laughing as hard as I was.

After the hilarity died down and we still faced the sky, our dicks flapping in the wind, raindrops spattering around us, Breck reached for my hand.

"I'm sorry."

"Me too."

Still, we didn't move. Weird that it almost seemed…peaceful.

"You were wrong," I said after a bit.

"About what?"

"About my house bein' a sanctuary filled with memories of Mick." I turned my head and looked at him to find he was already looking at me. "Mick never lived here."

"I thought you lived together."

"We did. Just not in this house. I had a trailer. After Mick died…I got rid of it. Then I bought this. It's one of those pre-fab modular homes that's built on site, but I still ended up doin' a ton of work on it—"

Breck loomed over me. "Why didn't you tell me?"

"You never asked." I brushed his sodden hair off his forehead. "So it really was just a stupid oversight that you've never been in my house or in my bed. Would you like to come in and see my place?"

"I'd love to." He smiled and then he winced. "You have a first aid kit? Because I'm pretty sure there's gravel embedded in my knees."

"Yeah, my elbows are feelin' a little raw." I kissed his smirking mouth. "But it was worth it."

"Definitely."

Chapter Nine

Breck

Somehow we dragged our sodden, love-drunk asses into the house.

I didn't look around. I'd have plenty of time for that later. Years, I hoped.

Neither of us lingered beneath the spray of hot water when we had the option of curling up in Cres's warm, dry bed.

Probably made me a prick, but I had a surge of satisfaction knowing I was the first—and only—man Cres would share this space with.

No surprise we dozed off after the intensity of the storm we'd dealt with.

But as soon as Cres stirred, half-awake in that sleepy-eyed state, I took him again. Face to face, our hands clasped together above his head.

It was a sweet reconnection.

It was a necessity that I could show him my loving side I'd never shared with another man. He accepted that part of me without a moment's hesitation. I whispered the words I'd held inside my heart and he whispered them back with equal conviction.

I came when he did, my name spilling from his lips as I poured everything of myself into him—my heart, my body and my soul.

Afterward, Cres had sprawled on his stomach beside me.

I couldn't help but trace the scratches I'd left on his back. "So…it's later."

"And?"

"And…can we talk about a couple of things?"

"Of course I'll let you fix supper in my kitchen. In fact, head out there right now and get crackin'."

I pinched his ass and he swore at me.

"Fine. What's on your mind?"

"The first session ended at Grade A day before yesterday."

"I know. What's that mean?"

"I'm not sure if I'm cut out to teach, but there's no rush for me to sign a contract."

"Why not?"

"The Gradskys are numbers people. They have to assess and reassess, so they're delaying the second session until next spring. In the meantime, I did sign on to head up the soil prep and organic certification process for Stirling's organic farming experiment."

Cres pushed up onto his elbow. "Really? I thought you were done with farming."

I shrugged. "I liked farming. I didn't like workin' with my family. So I'll be using my Ag degree for the first time since I graduated."

"That's exciting for you."

"But?"

He smirked. "But I'll take shit from my brothers for bein' involved with a *farmer*."

"Maybe they'll cut you some slack when they hear I'm offering to be your ranch hand until Wyn is back in action." I swept my thumb across the dark circle beneath his eye. "You can't continue to do this alone, Cres. If it's not me, you'll have to hire someone anyway, right?"

"Probably. But won't you be busy enough with your new job?"

"Macon and Stirling said I can set my own hours. I figured some days you'd need more help than others. On the slower days, I'll head to Grade A."

"But you'll be here at night?"

"Yep." I pecked him on the mouth. "I'm lookin' forward to sleeping with you the whole night."

"Me, too." Cres ducked his head, acting as if he was concentrating on smoothing out my chest hair.

"What else is on your mind?"

"If you're not workin' on Sunday, would you wanna go to Denver with me? I need to see for myself how Wyn is holding up and I want to meet Truman."

"I'd love to come along and let your family know that I'm not goin' anywhere. Think Wyn will be okay with us bein' together and with me helping out on the Grant Ranch?"

Cres looked up at me. "He'd better be okay with it since Mel worked as his ranch hand for a couple of weeks and that's how they ended up playin' house for real. This is just as real to me. Plus, I want you to meet my Mom and Dad." He snickered. "Our nephews will wear you out. They are wild. It's so fun riling them up and then handing them back to their folks. I'm betting Tru will be the same way."

Everything he'd said after *our nephews* was hazy.

He had no idea the power those words had for me.

Our.

He was mine and I was his.

I almost felt my feet getting heavier, as if they were finally ready to set down roots.

"Breck? You okay?"

I looked at him and grinned. "Fuck, yeah. Never been better."

* * * *

Also from 1001 Dark Nights and Lorelei James, discover Roped In and Stripped Down.

Sign up for the 1001 Dark Nights Newsletter
and be entered to win a Tiffany Key necklace.

There's a contest every month!

Go to www.1001DarkNights.com to subscribe.

As a bonus, all subscribers will receive a free
1001 Dark Nights story
The First Night
by Lexi Blake & M.J. Rose

Turn the page for a full list of the
1001 Dark Nights fabulous novellas...

Discover 1001 Dark Nights Collection Three

HIDDEN INK by Carrie Ann Ryan
A Montgomery Ink Novella

BLOOD ON THE BAYOU by Heather Graham
A Cafferty & Quinn Novella

SEARCHING FOR MINE by Jennifer Probst
A Searching For Novella

DANCE OF DESIRE by Christopher Rice

ROUGH RHYTHM by Tessa Bailey
A Made In Jersey Novella

DEVOTED by Lexi Blake
A Masters and Mercenaries Novella

Z by Larissa Ione
A Demonica Underworld Novella

FALLING UNDER YOU by Laurelin Paige
A Fixed Trilogy Novella

EASY FOR KEEPS by Kristen Proby
A Boudreaux Novella

UNCHAINED by Elisabeth Naughton
An Eternal Guardians Novella

HARD TO SERVE by Laura Kaye
A Hard Ink Novella

DRAGON FEVER by Donna Grant
A Dark Kings Novella

KAYDEN/SIMON by Alexandra Ivy/Laura Wright
A Bayou Heat Novella

STRUNG UP by Lorelei James
A Blacktop Cowboys® Novella

MIDNIGHT UNTAMED by Lara Adrian
A Midnight Breed Novella

TRICKED by Rebecca Zanetti
A Dark Protectors Novella

DIRTY WICKED by Shayla Black
A Wicked Lovers Novella

A SEDUCTIVE INVITATION by Lauren Blakely
A Seductive Nights New York Novella

SWEET SURRENDER by Liliana Hart
A MacKenzie Family Novella

For more information visit www.1001DarkNights.com.

Discover 1001 Dark Nights Collection One

FOREVER WICKED by Shayla Black
CRIMSON TWILIGHT by Heather Graham
CAPTURED IN SURRENDER by Liliana Hart
SILENT BITE: A SCANGUARDS WEDDING by Tina Folsom
DUNGEON GAMES by Lexi Blake
AZAGOTH by Larissa Ione
NEED YOU NOW by Lisa Renee Jones
SHOW ME, BABY by Cherise Sinclair
ROPED IN by Lorelei James
TEMPTED BY MIDNIGHT by Lara Adrian
THE FLAME by Christopher Rice
CARESS OF DARKNESS by Julie Kenner

Also from 1001 Dark Nights

TAME ME by J. Kenner

For more information visit www.1001DarkNights.com.

Discover 1001 Dark Nights Collection Two

WICKED WOLF by Carrie Ann Ryan
WHEN IRISH EYES ARE HAUNTING by Heather Graham
EASY WITH YOU by Kristen Proby
MASTER OF FREEDOM by Cherise Sinclair
CARESS OF PLEASURE by Julie Kenner
ADORED by Lexi Blake
HADES by Larissa Ione
RAVAGED by Elisabeth Naughton
DREAM OF YOU by Jennifer L. Armentrout
STRIPPED DOWN by Lorelei James
RAGE/KILLIAN by Alexandra Ivy/Laura Wright
DRAGON KING by Donna Grant
PURE WICKED by Shayla Black
HARD AS STEEL by Laura Kaye
STROKE OF MIDNIGHT by Lara Adrian
ALL HALLOWS EVE by Heather Graham
KISS THE FLAME by Christopher Rice
DARING HER LOVE by Melissa Foster
TEASED by Rebecca Zanetti
THE PROMISE OF SURRENDER by Liliana Hart

Also from 1001 Dark Nights

THE SURRENDER GATE By Christopher Rice
SERVICING THE TARGET By Cherise Sinclair

For more information visit www.1001DarkNights.com.

About Lorelei James

Lorelei James is the *New York Times* and *USA Today* bestselling author of contemporary erotic romances in the Rough Riders, Blacktop Cowboys, and Mastered series. She also writes dark, gritty mysteries under the name Lori Armstrong and her books have won the Shamus Award and the Willa Cather Literary Award. She lives in western South Dakota.

Connect with Lorelei in the following places:

www.LoreleiJames.com

www.Facebook.com/LoreleiJamesAuthor

www.Twitter.com/LoreleiJames

www.Instagram.com/LoreleiJamesAuthor

Discover More Lorelei James

Roped In
A Blacktop Cowboys® Novella

Ambition has always been his biggest downfall...until he meets her.

World champion bulldogger Sutton Grant works hard on the road, but his quiet charm has earned the nickname "The Saint" because he's never been the love 'em and leave 'em type with the ladies. When he's sidelined by an injury, he needs help keeping his horse in competition shape, but he fears trying to sweet-talk premier horse trainer London Gradsky is a losing proposition--because the woman sorta despises him.

London is humiliated when her boyfriend dumps her for a rodeo queen. What makes the situation worse? She's forced to see the lovebirds on the rodeo circuit every weekend. In an attempt to save face, London agrees to assist the notoriously mild, but ruggedly handsome Sutton Grant with his horse training problem on one condition: Sutton has to pretend to be her new boyfriend.

But make believe doesn't last long between the sassy cowgirl and the laid-back bulldogger. When the attraction between them ignites, London learns that sexy Sutton is no Saint when that bedroom door closes; he's the red-hot lover she's always dreamed of.

The more time they spend together, the more Sutton realizes he wouldn't mind being roped and tied to the rough and tumble cowgirl for real...

* * * *

Stripped Down
A Blacktop Cowboys® Novella

Never challenge a cowboy to a little naughty competition…

A flirty game of sexual truth or dare between best man, Wynton Grant, and maid of honor, Melissa Lockhart during their BFF's wedding reception results in a steamy hookup.

But their plans for a *one and done* change when a family crisis leaves Wyn shorthanded at the Grant Ranch. Experienced horsewoman Mel volunteers to help out and gets way more than she bargained for living under the same roof as the sexy rancher. Playing house has never appealed to Wyn…until now.

But the feisty redhead is keeping secrets and Wyn's not above stripping her bare—body and soul—to get to the bottom of it…

On behalf of 1001 Dark Nights,

Liz Berry and M.J. Rose would like to thank ~

Steve Berry
Doug Scofield
Kim Guidroz
Jillian Stein
InkSlinger PR
Dan Slater
Asha Hossain
Chris Graham
Pamela Jamison
Jessica Johns
Dylan Stockton
Richard Blake
BookTrib After Dark
The Dinner Party Show
and Simon Lipskar

Made in the USA
Las Vegas, NV
22 March 2021